UNEXPECTED

Warren C. Holloway

GOOD 2 GO PUBLISHING

UNEXPECTED
Written by Warren C. Holloway
Cover Design: Davida Baldwin, Odd Ball Designs
Typesetter: Mychea
ISBN: 978-1-947340-74-9
Copyright © 2021 Good2Go Publishing
Published 2021 by Good2Go Publishing
7311 W. Glass Lane • Laveen, AZ 85339
www.good2gopublishing.com
https://twitter.com/good2gobooks
G2G@good2gopublishing.com
www.facebook.com/good2gopublishing
www.instagram.com/good2gopublishing

PROLOGUE

"Oh my God! Holy shit! What are you doing?" The college fraternity student asked as he ran fast, trying to evade punishment from me.

"No need to run, young man. This will all be over soon. Then you'll join the rest of your friends." I ran behind him with a smile, loving the rush I was getting, knowing that he was fearing for his life, a life that was soon to be in my control. The completion of a project, it is always satisfying, yesss, it is. His breathing was nimble, and I could hear the oxygen being vacuumed into his mouth and lungs, only to be forced out, to fuel his attempt to flee. It's as if he was right by my side, close, intimate, and ready to die. His feet pounded into the pavement wanting to get away, not realizing the alcohol he drank was tainted with tranquilizer, so soon, his body would shut down as I wanted it to. Yesssss, the thought alone excited me, giving off a sadistic euphoric pleasure of malice. College boy's racing heart assisted my work of art, pumping the fluid through his already patulous

veins, causing his muscles to relax with no movement. Then suddenly, it started to happen. His body
was shutting down.

"Oh no, no, no!" he pleaded frantically, sensing
the sudden change in his body as he hit the ground
hard. His grunts and moans could be heard, but to
no avail. No one was going to save him now. He was
temporarily paralyzed yet aware of what was to
come. This alone was giving me the rush of murder,
which is more pleasurable than a night of passion
with a cheap whore.

"Now, now, you're just as guilty as the others,
young man," I said as I came closer, seeing fear in
his eyes. I felt like God, but more diabolical, ready to
take his life in an unforgiving way. I could see in his
eyes he was praying to escape this day and very
moment, but it was too late.

ONE

The city was covered with snow, enhancing the mood for the holiday season, allowing those that choose to celebrate feel even more jolly with this white Christmas. John Davis Senior was one of those in the holiday spirit. The young Afro-American came from nothing, until he finally chose the right path, investing his money into a chain of stores he was now a proud owner of. He was five foot eleven and medium built, with dark hair, brown eyes, and a smile his wife Diane loved. John, being a grateful person, was always willing to give back to those in need, something he chose to do today as he exited the East Mall and donated to the Salvation Army Santa Claus. John made sure he got all of the gifts for his son and wife: diamonds for her, Hulk Hogan action figure for his son, since he was his son's favorite wrestler. He made it to his Lincoln Town Car and placed the gifts inside. At the same time, he saw some kids throwing snowballs back and forth as they were walking to their car with their mother. Once inside, he turned the music on and listened to the Temptations Christmas album. As the music played, he drove home, reflecting on how it was for him as a kid this time of year, looking forward to seeing Santa and unwrapping gifts. It didn't take long before he pulled up to his home in the Bellevue area, with a three thousand-square-foot brick home, fireplace, lower lounge, and game room. His wife, Diane, was a five-foot-eight brown-skin beauty with a radiant smile, long black hair that reached the middle of her back, and glowing hazel brown eyes that seemed to light up when she saw him. She stood in the doorway to greet her man as he pulled into the driveway. He smiled when he saw her as he grabbed the bags in the trunk. "Dee Dee, you can come out and help a brother with these bags," he said, not really needing his wife's help.

"With those muscles, you don't need my help, just my love and support," she responded, making him smile, shaking his head, happy to see his wife.

"Where's junior at?" he asked.

"In his room doing homework."

"Good, I can hide these gifts downstairs, and don't be trying to peep at what they are either."
"What if I act surprised when I open the gifts?" she said, being funny. He didn't respond, taking the gifts downstairs. Once he was in the basement, she called out to her son. "Junior! Junior your dad is home!" It didn't take long before he came down from his room.

Moments later John Sr. came up from the basement, over to his son, throwing his hands up in a playful boxing manner. "Let's go, champ," Senior said.

"Okay, I'm Ali, and you're Joe Frazier, Dad," Junior said, throwing punches with the sound effects behind them. Then Senior let his ten-year-old son land a punch so he could go down. "Down goes Frazier. I win, Dad," he said with excitement.

"I want a rematch. I demand a rematch," Senior said. "I smell some good cooking, babe," Senior said.

"A little soul food my way, with love," she said looking on at her husband and son. "It'll be ready in ten minutes, so make sure you two wash your hands before you come in my kitchen, or I'll be Mike Tyson and knock you both out," she said, making them laugh as she turned and headed back into the kitchen. John loved his wife and all she did for him and his son. Diane, being thirty-two, was three years younger than John, but the same age in love. John spent the next ten minutes with his son before they cleaned up and made their way into the eat-in kitchen where the soul food spread was, with ribs dripping with special sauce, fried chicken seasoned with spicy garlic, baked macaroni and cheese, potato salad, corn on the cob, blueberry corn bread, and fresh collard greens cooked with bacon.

"This food looks and smells like somebody loves us, Junior," he said, making his wife light up with a smile, feeling his appreciation for her hard work and time in the kitchen.

"Of course, Mommy loves us, right, Mom?"

"Yes, baby," she said, kissing him on the cheek.

They all took a seat to pray over the food before diving into this amazing food spread. At the same time, they enjoyed each other's presence and conversation. Diane was looking on at the two men she loved, who were appreciating her hard work and love she put into the food.

"Babe, you did a really good job with these ribs," Senior said. Before she could respond, a firm knock followed by the doorbell sounded off, getting their attention. Senior's head raised from his plate, and he licked the barbecue from his fingers as he sat the rib on the plate. "I wonder who that is? I'll get it. Don't eat all the ribs, Junior," he said, standing up and wiping his hands before going to answer the front door. He looked out the peep hole and saw it was two uniformed Harrisburg Police officers. "What do they want?" he wondered as he opened the door. They stood looking back at him as if he didn't belong in his own home, since this was a predominantly white area. His success had afforded him this place "How can I help you officers tonight?" John asked.

"We're here to speak with John Davis Senior."

"That's me. What seems to be the problem?"

"One of your stores was robbed this evening. The clerk was killed in the process. We need you to come over to the scene, ID the victim, and provide us with next-of-kin info," the officer said. John couldn't believe that someone would do such a thing, especially with it being the holiday season.

"I need to grab my coat, and I'll follow you guys over," he said, making his way back into the house.

His wife could see on his face that something is wrong. "What is it, baby?" she asked with concern in her voice.

"Something happened at one of the stores. Don't worry yourself. I'll be back for them ribs and fried chicken, so don't eat all of it, Junior," he said, kissing Diane on her soft, warm lips, briefly clearing his mind.

"Mmmh, dessert, I can't wait til you get back. I'll be waiting for you sexy man," she said, loving her husband.

"I guess I have to save you some of the ribs, huh, Dad? I won't eat them all anyway. It's a lot."

"That's good, because your mom would be up all night making more ribs if you didn't save me any," he responded.

"I have better things and ideas to be up all night for," she said with a smile and lust in her eyes for her man only.

He just laughed, giving her another brief kiss before heading out to the car. "I'll follow you officers to the store. Which one is it?" Senior asked.

"17th Street."

"I never had any problems over there, especially with the way I give back to the city," he said.

"The holiday season creates problems and desperation, backed with the drugs some of these people are on," the officer said. John got into his car with so many thoughts of seeing one of his employees murdered and having to explain this to their family. The pain and grief they'd experience, especially with Christmas days away. No family should have to go through this.

TWO

Within minutes they were pulling up to a now-crowded crime scene with homicide detectives and crime scene investigators present, along with those who lived in this area, all curious about what was going on, who, and why. As John entered the store, he could see the bullet-riddled coolers with the shattered glass everywhere.

"Mr. Davis, over here," the detective said, wanting him to ID the body. John made his way around the other side of the counter. Immediately he recognized the lifeless body and clerk from her engagement ring, since her face was marred from the slug that slammed into her face. The one half of her face that did remain had her eye intact, showing fear, as if she was pleading for her life. Her mouth was still open as if she had tried to scream.

"This is so wrong. Sarah Smith is her name, and she didn't deserve this," John said, choked up. "They could have taken everything in here and left her alive."

"We'll track down the son of a bitch that did this," the detective said. "We all need money for the holidays, but this isn't the way to get it."

"Mr. Davis, we're going to close this down to comb it for evidence. Oh, one more thing: you have cameras in this place?" the officer said.

"One over the entrance, the other over the register."

"That's great. This should point us in the right direction. Now Sarah's next-of-kin info."

"1415 Liberty Street, with her fiancé and kids."

"Thank you for coming out, sir. Be safe and enjoy the holiday season."

"I'll definitely try," John responded, heading out. He headed to the uptown area to another of his stores. He wanted to make sure his employees were safe and aware of what just took place. As he was driving over the Maclay Street bridge, he noticed a car stopped in the middle of the bridge with its hazard lights on, along with four young white males in their teens or early twenties, looking stranded and out of place stuck in the heart of the city, in the dark snowy night.

John knew it wasn't safe for them to be stuck like

this in the city, especially after what he had seen tonight at the store. So, he pulled up, rolling his window down, to see what was going on and what they needed. "Looks like you guys have a little problem," John said.

"Yeah, man, it died out on us. I think it's the battery. You got cables, man?" the college-age-looking kid asked.

"I do, so you're in luck. I'll help you get out of this cold," John said, being a good Samaritan. He pulled over, positioning his car closer to theirs to connect the cables. Then he hopped out, popping the trunk and the hood before getting the cables. "It's pretty cold out here, and having your battery die out here is a bitch," John said, extending the other end of the cables for them to take.

"Being out here is a bitch. Now get the fuck in the car, nigger!" the young boy said as they grabbed John, forcing him into the back seat of their car. With the sudden shift in their demeanor, accompanied by the force of four young college kids, he was shocked and overwhelmed at the same time. He flashed back to Sarah's lifeless body, so he didn't want to put up a fight, because he wanted to make it home to his family.

Now in the back seat in between two of the young males, he started to speak with hopes they would come to their senses. "You're making a bad mistake right now. You can let me out and go home and enjoy the holiday season with your families." They all remained silent until he continued on, "You will go to jail for this. Kidnapping is a federal offense!"

"Shut the fuck up, nigger, or I'll blow your fucking head off!" the one in the front seat said, turning around and pointing the gun in John's face. As they continued driving off, John's car sat with the hood up and the cable partially connected, with his hazard lights flashing in the winter night, slowly being covered up by the snow fall. John knew he could take each one of these kids, but at gunpoint, he didn't want to risk his life.

He needed to outsmart them, by using his brain. "How much money you all want? I own a string of stores. I can pay you whatever you want. Just pull over and let me out. I'll walk back to my car," he said, at the same time smelling the alcohol on their breaths. There was no reasoning with them at this point. "Is this some fraternity thing you have to do? If so, is it worth going to jail for?"

The kid in the front seat brought the .357 Magnum back into view, pulling the hammer back with his thumb. "I told you, nigger, don't say a word. We'll do what we got to do. When we're done, you can run back to your car."

The two kids John sat in the middle of didn't say a word, as if they were scared of the young kid in the front seat. Once the gun was lowered, they started to speak. "No one is ever going to believe we got a nigger from the city, so we had to bring him back for proof," the kid to John's right said, making him aware that he was a part of a fraternity challenge. The challenge was to scare him and take his car, not bring him back. These idiots being drunk wanted to impress the rest of their fraternity brothers. John didn't think highly of being captive or being called a nigger. Now he was thinking more in depth on how he was going to get out of this and bring these clowns to justice, making them pay for this kidnapping.

Back in Harrisburg, Diane was patiently waiting

on her husband to return home, so they could pick back up where they left off: dinner, then dessert her way.

THREE

The college fraternity boys were back at the frat house drunk and high from smoking marijuana. Now they had John secured with his legs tied to a chair, his hands bound behind him. They were forcing alcohol down his throat as someone held his nose, giving him no other choice. They were even mixing the 151 rum with 190-proof Everclear. It all burned his throat, angering him even more. "Let me go! This is enough!" John snapped, looking around at each of them.

"Shut up, nigger! We'll let you go when we're done!" one of the frat boys yelled out in between smoking.

"Untie me, and I'll kick all of your asses!"

"That's the alcohol talking, you dumb fuck," the frat boy standing at John's side said, taking a puff of the weed before blowing the smoke into John's face.

"This is some good shit right here, and just like this weed, I'll smoke your ass and drag you from the back of my car."

Hearing his words made John burn with anger. At the same time, he tried to headbutt the frat boy, but he moved away quickly. The frat boy laughed, pissing John off even more. "Everybody in here is going to jail! I got a good memory, and I can see all of you young punks' faces!" he snapped, sending the fear of them going to prison through their minds and bodies. He had seen each of their faces.

One of the frat boys was shaken at the thought of going to jail, so he snapped, throwing a bottle hard and fast at John. "No one is going anywhere, nigger!"

John turned toward the loudly shouting voice only to be greeted with the brute force of the bottle slamming into his face, knocking him unconscious, making his body slump in the chair, looking to be lifeless, as blood spewed out from his head. At the same time silence fell on the entire house as they all looked on at his limp body. Each of them feared the worst, that he might be dead. They couldn't have this, not here.

"Where's the four idiots that brought him here?"

"Me, the twins, and Mike."

"Get this scum out of here and back to the city where he belongs."

The four frat boys rushed over and untied John, panicking. "Oh shit, man. What the fuck did he throw the bottle for? We were just trying to scare him," the twin said.

"I don't know. Let's just get him back to where we found him," Mike said.

"Hey, you idiots, calm down. No one will ever know he was here, right?" the head frat boy said, looking around. They shook their heads in agreement. They carried John out to the car before driving back to Harrisburg on I-81. The silence in the car was a clear sign of their fear about how seriously things had turned out. Suddenly, John's groaning from the pain alerted the two in the back seat, since they thought he was dead.

"Holy shit, dude! He's fucking alive!" the twin said.

"Oh my God! This is like good and bad all at the same time, dude!" his brother said. Each of them knew he could snap if he woke up, especially after what they had done to him.

"We got duct tape in the trunk. Pull over!" the frat boy in the front seat said. The car came to an abrupt halt on the side of the road. One of the twins jumped out, retrieving the duct tape, before returning quickly, nervously shaking, trying to secure John's ankles.

"Hurry up, bro."

"Don't fucking rush me. I got this!" Just as those words flowed from his mouth, John's eyes opened, as he could feel tugging on his feet. At the same time he realized he was no longer in the frat house. He also noticed his hands were free, so he started punching the kid in the head that was trying to secure his legs. His twin brother, seeing this, was trying to pull John off of him, to no avail, in his anger and strength.

"Help! Help us! Get this fucking nigger off of me!" the twin yelled out. John, now gaining the advantage over them, wanted to make them pay for what they did to him. The frat boy in the front passenger seat saw that the twins were getting their asses kicked, so he pulled the .357 Magnum out.

Hearing the ignorance of the frat boy in the front seat only made John go even harder to fight for his life and freedom. The twins were shouting in fear, feeling his adult power and anger taking them over. Suddenly, ceasing all movement, the roaring of the .357 Magnum sounded of as two thunderous rounds slammed into John's flesh, sucking the life from his body, robbing him of any more chances to fight or be free. The first round breached his heart, and the other his lung, killing him instantly.

Everyone inside of the car was now terrified, except for the shooter. He was feeling the power and the rush of murder. "Dude! Dude, what the hell did you do that for, dumbass!" the driver asked, sobering by the second, fearing the reality they were about to face with a body in the back seat.

Jason Estill, the shooter, was a young nineteen-year-old, standing six foot even, with a medium build and weighing close to two hundred pounds. He turned to Michael Smith, the driver, who was twenty years old and a six-foot-two basketball player, with black hair and gray eyes that were sketchy.

"I did it because he was kicking their asses. What

did you have in mind?" Jason said.

"What did I have in mind? What, are you retarded or something? He's dead now, so what's your plan?"

Jason stared at Michael, sizing him up as he clenched his gun in hand. Ricky Jones and his twin brother Ronnie were both blond-haired kids standing five foot eleven. They were in shape, with young model looks and glowing blue eyes the girls on campus loved. The twins were now scared to death, never seeing anyone shot or having a dead body up against their flesh, freshly murdered.

"I don't want to go to jail, man. You should have helped instead of killing him," Ronnie said, shaking.

"No one is going to jail, so stop acting like a fucking pussy!" Jason said, then added, "Dump his body over there on the side of the road."

The twins pulled his body out of the back seat. Blood streaking on the seats out into the snow, they drug him across to the edge of the woods.

"This is far enough, Ronnie. Let him lie here. Someone will find him in the morning," Ricky said as they made it back to the car. At the same time a Pennsylvania State Trooper was pulling up behind their car, assuming they were stranded on this snowy night. When the twins saw the trooper, their hearts started racing faster than they were when they were struggling with John kicking their ass.

"This is not good, bro. I don't want to go to jail," Ronnie said. The trooper exited his car, making his way to the car. At the same time, so many thoughts entered the twins' minds. Should we turn and run? We can point the finger at Jason, the shooter. It would look bad either way with them walking away from the body.

As the twins got closer to the car, the trooper noticed them approaching, so he became curious. "Is everything okay, gentlemen? Are you guys stuck?" Trooper Holmes made his way to the driver's side to question the driver as is normal procedure to determine if help was needed. He flashed his light into the car, and he saw two other occupants. At the same time his trooper instincts kicked in, giving him even more reason to want to question these young men. "You young men in here okay?"

Jason was still drunk, feeling the buzz and the rush of murder as he clenched the .357 Magnum off to the side, out of the trooper's sight.

"Yes, yes, sir, everything is okay. We pulled over 'cause my buddies couldn't hold it any longer." Michael's attempt to divert the trooper backfired, with his breath reeking of alcohol and the smell of marijuana on their clothing.

"How many drinks you had tonight?" the trooper asked. Trooper Holmes, a seven-year veteran, could sense these young men were trouble. It was displayed in their demeanor and on their faces, accompanied by the smell of alcohol.

"No drinks, sir, not us," Michael responded.

"Let me see your driver's license and registration, please? "As those words flowed from his mouth, the twins opened the back door, making the interior light come on, exposing the blood-saturated back seats with a trail of blood leading out of the car. Suddenly the trooper's adrenaline spiked. Going into his years of training, he reacted fast, reaching for his sidearm. At the same time, Jason was raising the .357 Magnum and squeezing off, hitting him twice and thrusting his body back with brute force, slamming his body down on the side of the highway in the snow. The twins jumped in, mentally and emotionally shaken as if they were in a bad nightmare. As the car was racing down the highway, Jason had this sadistic smirk on his face as images of the trooper's body being thrust from the slugs entered his mind.

"This is the fucking problem-solver, man!" Jason said, waving the gun around.

"Problem solver? You shot a fucking cop!" Michael snapped with his foot to the gas pedal, wanting to get away far and fast.

The twins were also losing it in the back seat. "Were all going to jail now!" Ricky blurted out in fear.

"This is bullshit, man! I'm not going down for your stupid-ass actions, Jason!" Ronnie said, then added, "I'm definitely telling them I didn't have anything to do with this if we get caught. I'll tell them you were a drunk loose cannon who lost his fucking mind!"

Jason turned around calmly, gun in hand, his eyes filled with evil and darkness. "You're not going to jail or anywhere, you piece of shit," he said, bringing the gun into view without hesitation. He squeezed the trigger, sending an unforgiving slug crashing into Ronnie's face, snapping his head back violently as chunks of his skull and brains ejected out the other side. The unexpected murder of his twin brother, accompanied by the warm blood splatter that sprayed him, sent Ricky into shock, traumatized and in fear for his own life.

Jason shifted the gun into Ricky's face. "Do you feel the same as your brother?" Ricky was speechless, staring down the barrel of the gun. "I thought so. I'm not going to jail," Jason said before turning back around.

***

Back on I-81 Trooper Holmes was thanking God for his bulletproof vest that stopped those two .357 Magnum slugs at close range. He also radioed in shots fired, along with the description of the car, and four occupants that were armed and dangerous. Multiple units responded to his location, as well as an all-out search for the Chevy Nova. Trooper Holmes also noticed the trail of blood leading over by the edge of the woods. He and the troopers investigated, finding the identification of John Davis

Senior. They also noticed he was wearing a wedding band, making him a family man that wasn't going to make it home tonight. Corporal Chimentez took the lead on this case. He would bring a close to this homicide case and shooting of one of his own officers. These young punks would be put in jail forever, once he tracked them down.

FOUR

Diane Davis was asleep on her couch, unaware of what had taken place with her husband. As far as she knew, he was out with the police checking all of the stores. A firm knock followed by the doorbell ringing woke her. She sat up clearing her eyes, looking over at the grandfather clock. Seeing the time sent an alarming fear through. She wondered who it could be, since her husband was still out. She made her way to the front door, hearing more knocking that seemed to be louder than the first round of knocking, adding to the fears and thoughts she was having. "Here I come, damn it!" she snapped as she came up to the door and looked out the peep hole. Two state troopers were standing on the other side of the door. She opened the door with concern. "What's wrong?" She cut straight to it. With it being two in the morning with her husband still not home, the holiday spirit was clearly sucked from her mood.

"Ma'am, are you the wife of John Davis Senior?" the trooper asked, seeing her wedding band.

"Yes, I am. Now what's wrong?" she asked, getting this bad vibe. "I'm sorry to tell you, ma'am, but your husband was murdered, and we—"

She screamed, cutting the trooper off. "What? What do you mean murdered? He was just here eating dinner with us," she said in disbelief that only a few hours ago, she was sitting across from him. "No! No! No! This can't be happening. Please tell me this is a mistake. You have the wrong house!" she cried out, dropping to her knees as her eyes filled with tears that seemed to burn with pain as they poured out. The troopers were trying to comfort her, but to no avail, as she pulled away from them, wanting this not to be true, wanting them to go away, as if it would make her husband come back home. Diane didn't realize her screaming and crying had jolted John Jr. out of his sleep. He came running down the steps over to his mom. "Mom, Mom, are you okay? Why are you crying?" he asked, looking down at her and then back up to the troopers.

The questions made her feel even more pain, knowing she would have to explain this to her son. She would have to tell him he had lost his father and best friend. The thought of this was tearing deep into her. She managed to look up at her son, who was trying to wipe her tears away. "Baby, Mommy is in pain and very sad right now." She thought she could tell him right then, but it didn't come out.

"Don't be sad, Mom. I love you, and my dad loves you too," he responded innocently, still unaware of his father's demise.

It took some time before she gathered herself enough to leave with the troopers to ID her husband's body. "Junior, go get dressed. We have to go somewhere with these troopers."

"Sneakers or boots, Mom?"

"Whatever you like, just hurry up, baby." As soon as he ran up the steps, she wanted to know more about what took place. "Did you see my husband yet? Is it bad? Did you catch the person responsible?" she questioned with hopes of finding comfort in their answers.

"Briefly we saw him, until we were directed to

come here to inform you. As for the suspects, they're closing in it now," he said, trying to keep what he knew to a minimum.

"So, they know who did this? Why did they hurt my husband?" she asked.

"Ma'am, we want to comfort you as much as possible, even answer your questions to an extent. However, details at this point will further anger you and bring you pain. It will also compromise the investigation," the trooper expressed to her, with hopes she wouldn't ask any more questions. She would never be done asking questions as long as the killer or killers were out there. Junior came back down ready to leave, at the same time wondering where his dad was, while at a loss for where they were going at this time of night. They exited the house, getting into the squad car with the troopers. The ride to the morgue was quiet, outside of some radio chatter. Diane was having so many thoughts about why and how this could have happened to her husband, none of which would bring him back.

FIVE

D iane was in the basement where the morgue
was. It had a chilling, eerie feeling of death
and unsettled souls, lost down here. They
pulled John's body out of the cooler, and at the same
time, Diane's heart was pounding, knowing she was
about to see her husband's lifeless body. They
unzipped the body bag, exposing his face. She
sucked in a chilled breath as her eyes widened, trying
to find the words to express what she was feeling, but
nothing. Only tears flowed from her eyes, falling
onto her husband's cold flesh and marred face where
the bullet had hit him. Now the blood was dried,
looking to be frozen in place. She leaned over,
kissing his face while holding his cold hand, flashing
back to their last moment shared at dinner, how she
wanted their night to end. Not like this.

"Ma'am, I take it this is your husband?"

"Yes, this is my husband. They took him away

from me and his son. They need to pay for this."

"Ma'am I assure you the troopers on this will not sleep until each of them is in custody," the trooper said, thinking about this murder as well as the attempted homicide on one of their own.

"My husband didn't deserve this," she said, letting his cold hand go and placing another kiss on his cold cheek. "I love you, baby. They will pay for this," she said in pain, wanting revenge, wanting to make them pay in every way. "God is going to make them all suffer tenfold. I'll see you again when my times comes," she added, stepping away from his body, wiping her tears away and regaining control over her emotions. She knew she had to be even stronger now, for her son, being the mother and father figure.

"Mrs. Davis, we'll be in contact, updating you on this case as it comes together, as we track the suspects down," the trooper said.

She nodded as she exited, walking over, and embracing Junior as if her husband told her to give him one last hug for him. "My dad's in a better place now, Mom," he said, figuring out what took place, being in a hospital.

SIX

A Pennsylvania State trooper came across the aban-doned gray Chevy Nova all the state and local police were in search of. The car was on Cameron Street, on the side of the road, close to the Farm Show Complex. Jason and the others scrambled to a pay phone after ditching the car, not realizing where they left the car wasn't too far from the troopers' barracks. The trooper also noticed as he came up on the car that there was someone inside. "Hands! Let me see your hands!" he yelled out, with his sidearm in hand, aimed at the person in the back seat. He came around to the side of the car, getting a visual, clearly seeing the person inside was deceased, from a gunshot to the face. He holstered his weapon, calling it in. It didn't take long before multiple units were present, combing the area and car, searching for identification for this victim inside, and running the tags on this Chevy Nova.

Within minutes, the dispatch came over the radio

with information on the car. "Trooper Marlo, this car is registered to a Maria Smith of Mechanicsburg, Pennsylvania."

"Dispatch, I'm going to need an address, so we can speak with Maria Smith about her car being here."

"512 South Market Street."

"Ten-four, dispatch."

Maria Smith was Michael's mother. She got the car for him for school. She never would have thought it would become a crime scene. Trooper Marlo memorized the name and address before directing troopers to this location. "Gentlemen, I'm going to need a team out to 512 South Market Street, in Mechanicsburg. Lock it in. This is our potential armed and dangerous suspect. We have one dead and a trooper shot, so stay sharp, men."

"Shoot to kill or capture, sir?" a young trooper questioned, knowing the suspect shot Trooper Holmes.

"We're going for an arrest and to make it home to our families. Nothing will get in the way of that," Trooper Marlo responded.

As troopers and homicide detectives secured this crimes scene, the other troopers headed to Mechanicsburg. The detectives found a school ID in the pants pocket of the kid in the back seat.

"Jesus, Ronnie, what happened to make someone do this to you, kid?" the detective said, then passed the ID on to the troopers. They would have someone reach out to his family and the school, to see what they could find out in regard to him being murdered in this back seat. Trooper Holmes was with Corporal Chimentez, a by-the-book, thirty-nine-year-old ex-marine standing six foot even and weighing 190 pounds. He'd been working as a trooper for the past eight years and was a well-groomed individual who paid attention to every detail and things that stood out, allowing him to crack down on criminals and close cases.

As soon as they came up on the car, Trooper Holmes flashed back to see these young punks that shot him. "This is definitely the car the I pulled up on with the shooter in it." Trooper Holmes was a six-foot-two Afro-American signing a fit 230 pounds. His clean-shaven bald head and face made him look younger than forty.

"From the looks of things, this guy got left behind, because he may have been the weakest link that would bring them all down," Corporal Chimentez said as he scanned the inside of the car.

"He's one of the boys that was outside of the car walking up as I approached," Trooper Holmes said, remembering what he was wearing.

"They did this kid in at point-blank range, with his brains on the back window like that. The shooter, from the looks of things, isn't going to go quietly when we do track him down. Two dead and the attempt on your life, we have to get him when he's least expecting it."

"Being honest, sir, I hope our guys take him down for what he did to me and these victims. A life sentence in jail isn't enough for a monster like that," Trooper Holmes said, really wishing he could be the one to pull the trigger on this young punk that shot him.

"I want to round up everyone connected to this case," Corporal Chimentez said, stepping away from the car. Then he added, "Trooper Holmes said there were four of them, minus this one inside, so we're looking for three suspects that are clearly armed and dangerous. Find out who they are, who their friends are, outside of this guy in the back seat. I want to know what caused this sudden violent rage and if they plan more acts of inane violence. I want these idiots in custody before more bodies are found," he said, making his way to his car, not having to repeat himself to the troopers standing around.

SEVEN

State troopers were closing in on the suburban home of Maria Smith in search of answers and a tentative suspect for murder and attempted murder. Six squad cars secured the immediate area, and troopers surrounded the two-story brick home, covering angles and exits in case things turned hostile. The tension was high, knowing a fellow trooper had been shot. Each step toward the house seemed to add emotions of anger, fueling this tense situation as the troopers gripped their sidearms, scanning the windows and doors. Michael was in his room blasting his new Metallica record as if nothing ever took place overnight. Maria was in the living room watching a Christmas special when she heard the knock on the door, which seemed hard and abrupt. She hurried to the door wanting to get back to her TV show. She opened the door see the troopers with serious faces and guns out.

"I would say Merry Christmas to you boys, but you don't look so happy," Maria said.

The troopers bypassed her remarks, focusing on one thing: their suspect. "Are you Maria Smith, the owner of a gray Chevy Nova?" the trooper asked firmly, breaking her Christmas spirit.

"Yes, I am. My son drives that car back and forth to college. I use the minivan right there," she said, pointing to the van in the driveway.

They briefly glanced over to the van. "Where's your son now?"

"He's upstairs listening to that crazy music. Can't you hear that crap? Come on in. I'm not heating up the whole neighborhood. I'll get him down here," she said, allowing them to come in as she went to the bottom of the steps to yell up to him. "Michael! Michael! Jesus, boy, you need to turn that nonsense down!" she said, becoming angry at her son as she walked upstairs to knock on his door.

He came to the door and saw his mom with a pissed-off look, so he turned the music down. "What now, Mom?"

"Don't what now me! Someone is downstairs wanting to speak with you!" she said, heading back downstairs. Michael came down seconds later, still bopping his head as if the music was playing. Maria was talking to the troopers, being nice and offering them the holiday cookies and candies she had made. As soon as Michael saw the troopers standing there talking to his mom, while another kept guard looking up at the stairs, awaiting his descent, his mind shot into overdrive, thinking the worst: jail. He couldn't go to jail, or for Jason's dumb-ass actions. His heart thumped as he came down off the step. Then it happened: he bolted toward the back door, running fast, at the same time catching the troopers off guard with his sudden sprint. They took off behind him, closing in, just as he opened the back door, only to be greeted with multiple guns aimed in his face.

"Get down! Get down! Don't you even think about making another move!" the trooper yelled out with his gun aimed at Michael. Each of them were pumped up, ready to take him out if he made a wrong move or reached for a weapon. They tackled him, taking him down hard to the floor, securing the cuffs tight as their adrenaline surged through their bodies. Michael could feel the cold steel of their barrels pressing against his head and body. Each of the troopers was ready to pull the trigger, since they felt he could be the one that shot their brother in arms.

"What the hell is going on here? Somebody better tell me something, in here jumping on my son!"

"Step back, ma'am. Your son is going to jail. Your car was involved in a cop shooting, as well as two homicides. One of the bodies is still inside your car," the trooper said.

"What? What are these cops talking about, Michael?" Maria asked, placing her hands on her hips, upset. Michael being silent wasn't helping; it only angered her. As they stood him to his feet, he still remained silent. Maria slapped him in his head. "This isn't how I'm supposed to spend my Christmas, Michael! Think about your sister, idiot!" she said, knowing she had to get a lawyer on this to help her son.

EIGHT

The team of state troopers reached the university in search of information about Ronnie Jones, their victim. They wanted to know why he was left behind like that and who the other three in the car with him were. All the students around, seeing multiple troopers, started becoming intrigued as to why these troopers were here. Ricky, Ronnie's twin brother, also noticed the fast-approaching, serious-looking troopers, so he slid off to his room with hopes of evading questions. Ricky was still traumatized by the events of last night that happened so fast and unexpectedly. He also feared what Jason's crazy ass could do to him, especially with the look he gave him after shooting his brother. It was like the devil himself was staring back at him. The trooper came up to the reception, placing the school ID on the counter. The receptionist looked at it and noticed the familiar face. "That's the twin, Ronnie. He and his brother are the pretty boys around here."

"Where do they stay?" the trooper asked, cutting to it.

"Down the hall to the left, room 109."

The troopers moved quickly toward the room. Their adrenaline spiked by the second as they closed in on the room, knowing two homicides had taken place along with an attempt on an officer's life. They wouldn't risk another officer being shot or any lives being lost today. Now at the dorm door, their guns were out and at the ready. They knocked on the door at the same time listening in to assess how many people were inside the room. Nothing and no one could be heard. Suddenly they could hear a thumping sound. Each of them was ready to move in, and they turned the doorknob and announced themselves. "Pennsylvania State Troopers coming in!" they said moving in with trained precision. "Ricky Jones, we need to speak with you about your brother, Ronnie!" the trooper stated with his gun out in front of him. "We advise you, kid, don't do anything stupid! Just come out slow with your hands visible, so we can get resolve and answers." The trooper continued to move through the dorm, heart racing, preparing for the unexpected with these wild kids, having no regard for life or consequences. As they turned the corner guns out, they were greeted with the sight of Ricky's body hanging and twitching as the life escaped his flesh. The troopers now knew what the thump sound was, from the chair he kicked out from underneath himself. They could see the fear in his eyes with ruptured veins in them—the fear of going to jail, the fear of Jason and his murderous ways. He enjoyed those shootings last night. The troopers also saw this lone tear escape down the side of his face that spoke volumes of his fears of being confronted by them. "Call this in. This kid obviously didn't have plans on going to jail or talking to us."

"We could have saved him, if only we were minutes earlier," Trooper Ross said.

"Don't beat yourself up about this, Ross. He committed this sin, in taking his own life. His guilt got the best of him," Trooper Banks said, not realizing his fears were deep and all too real. "Now I have to call Corporal Chimentez to make him aware of this sudden suicide."

This left Michael and Jason to face punishment for their volatile acts. Michael was now in custody, not willing to say a word to protect his friends, unaware Ricky had joined his twin brother in death.

NINE

Back over at the state trooper's barracks, Corporal Chimentez alongside Trooper Holmes was interrogating Michael Smith, wanting answers to their questions. "You think you're going to just sit there in that chair and not say a word? You better start talking now, before we round your buddies up and they start pointing the finger at you. We have two homicides and an attempted murder on a police officer. You will be lucky to get double life, instead of the death penalty, where you'll be electrocuted up at Rock View!" Corporal Chimentez snapped, wanting resolve. Trooper Holmes was standing on the other side of Michael, towering over him, wanting to bring him harm as they did in shooting him.

Holmes then moved behind Michael, placing his large masculine hands on his shoulders and aggressively squeezing down as he spoke intently, up close alongside his face. "You're a young punk trying to be tough with your silence. You ready to go to the big leagues in the state penitentiary? Mommy and Daddy or your punk-ass friends can't save you once you go there. So save yourself before it's too late," Trooper Holmes said, taunting him. He let his grip go and came around to the front of him, swiftly removing his sidearm, a .44 Magnum, and placing it to Michael's temple. "Is this what you really want, tough guy? How about I blow your fucking head off for shooting me?" he said, pulling the hammer back with his thumb. His sudden shift in interrogation caught Corporal Chimentez off guard too. Michael, also noticing the look on Chimentez face, knew this wasn't a game, but real.

"Trooper Holmes, put the gun down! Holster your weapon, Trooper!" Corporal Chimentez shouted to get control over this interrogation. Trooper Holmes had a breaking moment, flashing back to being shot. Chimentez saw this wasn't a bluff but all too real and could turn graphic quickly. "This kid isn't worth all you have, Trooper Holmes, so holster your sidearm." He pulled himself together, lowering and holstering his weapon and taking a step back, looking on at the now-shaken Michael Smith.

"Jesus Christ, man! I don't want to die. I'll tell you what you need to know. Just don't let him kill me," Michael blurted out.

Corporal Chimentez walked toward the door gesturing for Holmes to follow behind him, into the hall. Once outside of the room, he confronted his trooper. "You need time off to get your shit together, I can do that for you, because I can't have you ready to put a bullet in every suspect that comes into this station."

"I understand I got out of control a little, but I did what was needed before he lawyers up. His mom is in the other room making calls now, so we need to get names," Holmes responded.

"Let's go back in to see what he gives us," Corporal Chimentez said, leading the way, getting straight to it. "Who killed John Davis Sr.?"

"Jason shot him, trying to break up the fight between him and the twins."

"What's Jason's last name?" Chimentez asked.

"Estill, he's a fucking loose cannon, like he was loving the power the gun gave him. He even shot Ronnie because he said he was going to rat him out,"

Michael said, making them aware of why he was so silent, in fear of his own life.

"Mr. Davis was killed by the bullets. What about the duct tape and laceration above his eye?" Chimentez asked. Michael became the running water, spilling out the details, telling what took place from the beginning, how they were challenged to do this ridiculous act that went too far. Michael named fraternity members at the house who aided in this kidnapping and torture that led to murder.

"I've heard enough from this scum. Book him and take him to jail," Chimentez said before exiting the room, to direct his other troopers. "Gentlemen, I want this frat house shut down. I want all of the names on this paper rounded up. My main focus is the shooter, Jason Estill. He has killed two people in cold blood and attempted to take out one of our brothers in arms," Corporal Chimentez said, wanting resolve.

TEN

State troopers were closing in on the frat house, catching everyone off guard. "Get down! Get down!" They secured all of those involved with the hazing of John Davis Sr., the assault, and aiding in kidnapping. "What did we do wrong?" one of the frat boys asked, laying down on the floor after he was secured with cuffs.

"You're all under arrest for aggravated assault and kidnapping along with the harassment of John Davis Sr.!"

"I'm innocent! We didn't do anything!" another frat boy yelled out.

"Tell that to the courts. You're all going to jail for this. Which one of you is Jason Estill?"

"He's not here," the frat boy responded. Jason lived in Camp Hill, close to thirty minutes away.

Troopers present called this in to Corporal Chimentez, since he was leading the case. "Corporal

Chimentez, sir, Mr. Estill isn't at this location, he may be at his place in Camp Hill."

"Trooper Jacobs, bring the others in, get what detail you can out of them. I'll take care of the Estill kid," he said, ending the call before updating Trooper Holmes. "Our shooter is a no-show at school, so we're going to take a trip to his place, have a couple units follow for backup, in case things get out of hand."

"It will, at the rate this kid was going last night," Trooper Holmes said.

"He's sober now, thinking this morning, which explains why he didn't show up to school."

"Or hungover," Holmes said, gathering their things heading out.

***

10:34 AM

Chimentez and his team of troopers were now surrounding Jason's house. Chimentez was directing each of them into position before they approached the door, knowing this guy was the shooter, with deadly and murderous intent. Suddenly shifting everyone's attention, spiking their adrenaline, gunfire erupted from the second-floor window, roaring in this suburban area. Slugs slammed into the parked squad cars with force.

"I see you sons of bitches!" Jason yelled out from the window, unleashing a total of six shots before reloading.

He sat in the corner by the window, breathing heavy, his adrenaline spiked, his mind racing, not wanting to go to jail. He was thinking as long as he had his .357 Magnum with bullets in the box to keep reloading, he would fend them off, until he figured out an escape plan. Jason looked out the window, seeing the troopers now taking cover. "I'm not going to jail! I promise you this!" Jason yelled out, clenching the .357 Magnum, with his finger inside the trigger guard.

Chimentez looked over at the other troopers, his heart thumping, mind racing, processing how to unravel this kid without losing any more lives or risking any of his men being shot. "Jason, we came to talk with you about last night! No one has to go to jail or get hurt!" Corporal Chimentez said, trying to bring calm to this situation.

Jason fired two thunderous rounds, the first whizzing past Chimentez's face, pissing him off, the other shattering the squad car window. "I'm not stupid! You came here with all these troopers to arrest me!" He paused to scan the rest of the area, checking for movement. "It wasn't my idea to bring that nigger back to the frat house! We were challenged to do something crazy in the city! Shit just went really bad!"

Each of the troopers heard him speak and knew his fraternity antics had placed him in this bad position he was making worse with each bullet he fired off. Jason continued on rambling, in between looking out the window. Chimentez was now directing troopers to move in as he attempted to distract Jason. "I hear you're a smart student, Jason, so how did we get here?"

Jason seemed confused after drinking, using drugs, and staying up close to twenty-four hours—all things that were clouding his mental state. He even broke down crying, trying to process it all, now, how he got here to this point, as Chimentez asked. "I don't know! I can't go to jail, it's not for me," he said, looking down at the gun before reappearing back in the window. "I fucked up really bad!"

"We all make bad decisions, Jason. We have to learn from them. It's what makes us better as people!" Corporal Chimentez said.

"Oh God! God, please forgive me, for have sinned!"

"Move in now!" Chimentez directed, sensing this kid was about to make a bad decision he wouldn't live to regret. Jason fired off six rounds, catching one of the troopers moving in on the house. The other troopers returned fire, quickly proceeding to kick the front and back doors in. Jason took cover from the barrage of bullets coming his way. At the same time, he was reloading his gun, he could hear the troopers running up the steps. The end was near, for Jason, and he knew this with them kicking the door in, rushing into the room with guns out. Jason had the .357 Magnum pressed up against his temple.

"Put the gun down! You don't have to do this!" the trooper yelled out, looking on at Jason.

His eyes were dark and distant. His mind was made up. "I told you, I'm not going to jail!" he shouted out before forming a sadistic smirk and pulling the trigger. The abrupt roaring of the Magnum, accompanied by the brief force of the slug ejecting chunks of his skull and brains out, spraying the wall behind him, shocked them.

"Jesus Christ! He blew his fucking brains out!" the rookie trooper yelled out, never seeing anything like this. His training hadn't prepared him for something this graphic.

Corporal Chimentez came running into the house, up the stairs into the room, seeing the blood spatter. "This wasn't the easy way out. Heaven or hell, he has to answer for his sins of murder," Chimentez said, turning back around and heading down the steps. He instructed his troopers to secure the area until the coroner showed up. Now he was left with one person who was in the car with John Davis Sr. and Ronnie Jones before they were murdered. He was also present when Trooper Holmes was shot. Chimentez made sure the local news reporters were updated on this case and its arrest made, as well as those who had met their demise.

ELEVEN

A few days later, a funeral for John Sr. was underway at the Emanuel Baptist Church on 16th and Liberty Streets. Everyone was in all-black attire, but Diane chose to wear a cream-colored dress, not wanting to be in a deep, dark space like the all black made her feel. She wanted to celebrate her husband's life and legacy and their never-ending love. John Jr. was also wearing a cream dress shirt his mother had picked out for him. All of his friends and family came out to pay their respects, even those in the community he looked after when they were in need. Diane sat in deep thought as the preacher conducted the ceremony. "Today we're here to pay respects to one of God's children, John Davis Sr. God came to get his son, taking him home, because his work here on earth is done," the preacher said.

"Amen! Amen!" everyone said in the crowded church.

"I want you, John Jr., to know your father gave you his name to carry on his legacy. Although he is not physically present, he will always be here in you and watching over you. The love he gave you and your mother will always be present, allowing you to hold onto that memory of his affection, just like Jesus Christ has given all of us who believe his everlasting love."

"Amen! Preach!" Diane said, wiping the tear from the corner of her eye as the words sank in. At the same time, she wanted revenge, wanted a moment to pay respects,

"Take a moment to appreciate and understand why we're still here, because we all have a reason God is allowing us to walk his green earth."

"Hallelujah! Preach the word!"

The preacher continued on, giving his blessings to this going-away of John Sr. All came to a close, allowing those in attendance to view the body once more before closing the casket. John Jr. was at his mother's side, giving her as much comfort as a young boy his age can. This should never happen to any child.

TWELVE

June 1986
Dauphin County Court House,
Harrisburg, Pennsylvania

Six months had passed by since John Sr.'s murder. The honorable judge Joseph Klinefelter was preparing to sentence Michael Smith for his role in the murder. Diane was present along with John's family friends. "Mr. Smith, a jury of your peers found you guilty of second-degree murder. Would you like to say anything before I impose your sentence?" Judge Klinefelter asked. Michael stood looking over his shoulder, making eye contact with Diane, who seemed to be staring through him.

"I want to say to Mrs. Davis, I'm sorry for being a part of the events that led to your husband's demise. I wish I could take it all back, so you and your son could have him back." His plea for mercy through this spurious apology wasn't fooling anyone. Even his own lawyer was looking on at him taken back.

"Mr. Smith, you will not get mercy from this court, as I will impose a life sentence as stipulated within the guidelines, for your role in this case. With that said, you will be housed and fed by the Department of Corrections for the rest of your natural life without any chance of parole."

The sheriffs standing around closed in on Michael as he started snapping. "What the fuck you give me life for? I didn't even kill anybody! This is bullshit, you old bastard!" Michael shouted with evil eyes, not realizing his actions were being recorded by the stenographer as well as the local news reporters. The outburst also allowed the jurors to see they made the right decision. As he was being taken out of this courtroom, over in Judge Cherry's courtroom, the others that were present at the frat house hazing, aiding in kidnapping, were being sentenced to time served, parole, community service with cost and fines. Soon as Diane exited the courthouse, a slew of reporters closed in on her with questions, flying from every angle. "Mrs. Davis! Mrs. Davis, how do you feel about Michael's life sentence? Is it justice for your husband?"

"He got what he deserves. His outburst after sentencing made that clear. Yes, justice for my husband has been served."

"Mrs. Davis, how do you feel about the frat boys that got a slap on the wrist with time served and parole?" As the question flowed from the reporter's mouth, the frat boys came out of the courthouse.

Their presence angered Diane, stirring up tormenting emotions. However, she didn't display it, knowing the news cameras were rolling. "I don't really know what to say, other than maybe their punishment isn't going to jail."

"What exactly does that statement mean?" the reporter pried.

"The ground they walk on will be forever cursed, because God has control over all of us, and he doesn't like ugly," Diane strategically responded before walking away.

They continued yelling out questions as she left them standing alone. They started filling in the blanks reporting. "As you can see, Diane Davis is clearly disturbed by the light sentence the other frat boys received, in comparison to Michael Smith's life sentence. I'm Dale Wagner with Fox 43. Tune in for more local late-breaking news."

"Free? No one goes free! They're all guilty! Guilty! I almost lost it, but I stayed calm. No one deserves to be treated like this. The others escaped the real punishment, Ricky and Jason chose suicide, and Ronnie, they made of mess of him. Don't they know there's an art to this murder thing? Perfection is a must that gives the murdering of each victim a rush. The thought alone is making me excited, wanting to kill, kill, kill. Yesssss, they will get their punishment, no time served or community service here. There are four frat boys who think they got away, until they see me coming. I am the one. There will be none next to me." These murderous thoughts are streaming from someone deeply affected by this case, up close and personal.

***

Three weeks after the trial, Diane was at home on the couch watching TV, when the news came on displaying pictures of the frat boys involved in hazing her husband prior to his murder. She tuned in, turning the volume up and listening in. "Good evening, I'm Marlon Marks standing here on route I-81 next to the graphic sight of four young college frat boys, whose faces we all know from the recent murder trial. Now these young men lie here brutally murdered with evidence of torture in a strange fashion, yet left in a perfect line, side by side and bound. The troopers tell us this could be some type of cult or hazing gone bad." Diane muted the TV, having a silent moment, before Junior interrupted her.

"Are those the boys that hurt Daddy, Mom?"

"Yes, baby, it looks like they got themselves into a world of trouble," she said, turning the channel to the Cosby Show to change the mood with laughter. Diane, in between laughing at the show, was also laughing that the murdered frat boys had met their demise. Call it karma or coincidence, she still enjoyed it.

THIRTEEN

June 2, 1994
Harrisburg, Pennsylvania

Diane had found her little boy changing into a young man, soon to be nineteen, standing six foot even, looking more like his father, with his muscles from working out and playing sports. Junior was also ready to fulfill his father's legacy with the chain of stores that had grown over the years. He didn't want to do the college thing, with the success of the family business; he did it for his mom. He spent the summer going to different colleges feeling them out to see where he wanted to spend his four years. He even had his own place, giving him the privacy a young man his age needs, with girls and parties. His apartment had all the amenities, but his one prized possession was a large family portrait from when he was a kid, hanging right above the sofa. This picture was his daily motivation to succeed, to never let his mother or father down.

Today, after slowing down from partying and checking colleges out, he called his mom.

"Hello, Junior, how are things going with you?" she asked, happy to hear from her son.

"I'm doing fine, Mom, calling to see how you're feeling. I just came back from the search for college and the right girl to keep me company."

"Don't be worried about those girls. You just focus on education, the future outside of college."

"I know, Mom. I was just joking around. I'm focused on the real reason I'm here."

"I was a little worried about you, seeing the news with all those college kids across the state turning up dead on the side of the road, some left in their cars. You know, seeing that stuff reminded me—"

"Mom, Mom I'm okay. I won't leave the parties with any strangers. Besides, I'm a big boy now. I can handle myself or anyone who thinks they can take me," he said, looking on at his arms.

"Your dad could handle himself, too, but it didn't stop the bullets," she replied, wanting him to take his safety seriously. "I'll be safe and serious, Mom. I'll be over to see you later."

"I always cook good food, with love. I know you haven't eaten any good food running around all summer. So, I'll make your favorite: ribs."

"I'm ready to come over now just to watch the process and smell the aroma of the ribs and good cooking," he said, making her laugh.

"I love you so. See you when you get here."

"I love you, too, Mom," he said, hanging up the phone and smiling, thinking about the ribs and the memories of his father that bit brought. For him, it's as if his father was present when he was at the house for any meal. Junior made his way to his bedroom, where he started cleaning for the second time today, something he got from his mother, who cleaned all the time to keep her mind busy, after losing John Sr.

FOURTEEN

The summer months came to an end, and the new semester of college was beginning. Junior was at his apartment enjoying a turkey sandwich and chips while watching the six o'clock news, which was intriguing to him. He turned the volume up and saw the number thirteen in the caption. Thirteen college kids murdered in a fifty-mile radius. This made him think about his mom's words of being safe. These college kids clearly had met their demise not being safe. The thirteen victims also made nationwide news, as there were fears of a serial killer on the loose. The pressure of the media made law enforcement place restrictions on travel for the students with hopes of slowing the killings as they tracked this killer. Junior recognized the face of the trooper taking questions from the reporters. It was Chimentez, who was now a lieutenant.

"Lieutenant! Lieutenant! Do you have any leads on this pernicious serial killed that has murdered thirteen college students?"

"Lieutenant, how are these victims being targeted?"

"Could this be college hazing gone wrong?" A slew of reporters tossed questions in the air, hoping to get answers to him.

Lt. Chimentez was slightly overwhelmed by the barrage of questions. "Okay, people, one question at a time, if you want them answered!" he stated, taking control. "These victims are all college students, having the same pattern of death. As for leads, I cannot disclose this right now. We do recommend students follow our curfew imposed state-wide; also travel in pairs and be aware of your surroundings at all times."

"Lieutenant, will these victims' names be released? Also are there any clues or evidence left behind on the crime scenes?"

"The names of the victims will be held until we clear it with the families. As for evidence or clues left on the crime scene, I can't divulge that type of info right now."

"So, is that a yes, Lieutenant?"

He ignored the question and walked away, piquing their curiosity, making them want to know more.

FIFTEEN

The first semester was underway, and the students were rushing around to their classes, in between meeting new friends, all dressed to appeal to the opposite sex. John Jr. mingled with a few familiar faces from the parties over the summer. When lunch came, he took a break in the cafeteria with them. Those who didn't recognize him were curious about who he was, with his height, looking like he should be on the team.

"Dude, you look like you got a scholarship to play basketball. You got game or what?" one of the students asked.

John heard him as he was enjoying his lunch, at the same time being observant. "You talking to me?"

"Like, you're the only tall brother here. What brings you to Ship U?"

"Education is what we all came here for last I

checked," John responded, getting light laughter from the females at the table who were with the other students.

"Yeah, that's true, but you look like a ball-player."

"I got skills on the court, but that's not my focus. I have other things on my plate that are more important. What's your name, my man?" John asked, since he was questioning him.

"Kenneth Wilson, wide receiver and MVP last year," he said, bragging.

"I'll see you around, Kenny, maybe even drop you off in a one-on-one basketball game," Junior said, excusing himself from the table, heading back to his class.

As the day went on, he came across a female who caught his eye. She was nineteen years old, blond, and golden tan, with soft blue eyes and a smile that could be seen across the campus, just like her perky breasts, enhancing the rest of her beauty, standing five foot seven.

"Excuse me, I'm looking for the campus library, but if you can't find it, can you at least tell me your name, so this won't be a waste of time?" he said, trying to be smooth, making her laugh at his upfront approach and sense of humor.

"Okay, I have to admit that was the cutest introduction. My name is Elisabeth; my friends call me Liz."

"I'm John, my friends call me junior, which means we have to wait until we're friends to use each other's nicknames," he said, being funny. She picked up on his cuteness, visually and through conversation.

"I like you, John, a pretty boy that's pretty funny," she said.

Now he was smiling, appreciating her words that were stroking his teen ego. "You're beautiful, plus your eyes seem to glow."

"Thank you, no one has ever said that before," she said, running her hand through her hair and flipping it in a nervous yet flirtatious manner. Then she added, "Would you like to come to my party this weekend?"

"Sounds like we're getting off to a good start. Just tell me where."

"My mom's place. She's going out of town for the weekend."

"I'll be there. Give me the info."

She did just that. "Bring swim shorts, too. We have a pool, in case you want to get wet."

"I want to get wet with your sexy ass," he was thinking.

"I don't need trunks to get wet, but I'll bring them, so your girlfriends don't go crazy," he said, making her laugh, capturing the visual of his fit body wet, running around without shorts on.

"I'll see you then, unless we bump into each other again this week," she said, heading to her class, leaving him to take in the view of her from behind as she walked away.

SIXTEEN

State Troopers Barracks
Harrisburg, Pennsylvania

Lt. Chimentez was sitting at his desk reviewing the files of the thirteen murder victims, trying to come up with a connection, something that would point to the killer. As he flipped through the photos of the victims and crime scenes, a voice came through the air, getting his attention.

"We have another body!" the trooper yelled out, holding the phone in his hand. Lt. Chimentez stood up fast, as did the other troopers, alerted by the sound of another victim.

"Jesus Christ! This guy just won't stop!" Chimentez said, then added, "No time to play. I want guys on the scene right now. Get back to me as soon as they get there." The troopers scrambled out to I-81 while Lt. Chimentez focused back on the photos, trying to find errors. His desk was in a large cubical on the floor with the rest of his team. He leaned in, taking hold of his steaming cup of black coffee, no sugar or creamer. While he tended to the pictures, his officers closed in on I-81, seeing reporters already present, taking pictures, recording this graphic sight.

"We have to take control of this area before they contaminate it," Trooper Kincade said as they exited the car, pushing through the reporters.

"Get back! This is a crime scene, and you are all corrupting it, hindering an ongoing investigation. Which means I can take all of you to jail for obstruction!" he yelled out, getting their immediate attention. Each of them moved out of the way, at the same time questioning the troopers on this graphic crime scene.

"Troopers, can you tell us about this victim? Why are so many bodies being left along the sides of highways?"

"We can't answer your questions right now, because we have to assess and secure this area," Trooper Kincade said, looking on at the body, with the same pattern as the previous killings. Further search allowed them to know this is also a college student. Once they were done, they took questions.

***

"Can you tell us something about this crime scene that stands out to you?" the reporter asked, making him think they saw something he didn't.

"I can say it mirrors the previous murders, making this fourteen. This killer is one sick individual, wanting attention, as if this is a game or something. These are real lives being taken."

"Should the parents of students in college ask that their kids come home, instead of risking their lives, being out there?"

"They need to be safe wherever they are. Stay in groups like Lt. Chimentez said, along with following the curfew in place," he said, walking away and getting into his car, leaving the crime scene guys to do their job processing the body and scene. Once back at the barracks, they filled Lt. Chimentez in on the media being there first.

"So this serial killer is turning this into a media circus, to admire his murders?" Chimentez said.

"Sir, fourteen victims is not good. Shit is going to hit the fan, with the families putting pressure on us," Trooper Kincade said.

Before Chimentez could respond, Capt. Mosley a six-foot-two Afro-American, age fifty, came out of his office, interrupting with his deep voice booming through the air. "Enough is enough! Lieutenant, we're bringing someone in on this case to assist. I've already made the call to the bureau. They're sending someone from New York down to help."

"We're going to need the help with this killer thinking it's a game," Trooper Kincade said.

"This is far from a game. When you catch that son of a bitch, I want to have a face-to-face with him," Captain Mosley expressed. Chimentez was now feeling the pressure of having an outside agency come on this case. "Lieutenant, you and your men need to step it up. This state is relying on us, and America is watching."

"Failure is not an option, sir. We'll track this scum down," Chimentez responded, knowing with the FBI coming they'd pick this case apart, bringing it to a close, with or without their help.

SEVENTEEN

Two days later, the FBI sent out their best profiler to assist with closing this serial murder case that was getting attention nationwide. The profiler entered the barracks and got looks from the troopers noticing her striking beauty, standing five foot five, perfectly built, with a bronze tan from the Miami sun, having recently worked a case down there. Her long black hair was flowing, but her glowing green eyes sparkled as she walked with sophistication in each step, meaning all business, in her black dress with white top that showed her features with class. She instinctively scanned the room, seeing the men looking on at her, including Lt. Chimentez. He waved her over as he placed his sandwich down on his desk.

"I take it you know who I am?" she said.

"Your serious look and the way you're dressed say it all. Now what's your name?" Lt. Chimentez asked. "Samantha Barnes. I've been profiling for seven-plus years, assisting the closure of dozens of cases. I'm what we at the bureau call a closer."

"That's quite impressive. I hope you can be of assistance here; with the murders we have. I'm Lt. Chimentez, the old guy running the show when the captain is not around."

"Don't sell yourself short. You don't look that old. You just need rest from working long hours."

"Now down to business, I don't know how you work or where you want to start. These are the pictures I was looking on at with the victims from each crime scene," he said, sliding the photos over to her. She zoomed in and saw that they were all male, same age group, bound in identical fashion, even marks and lacerations in the same place, details that weren't made public thus far. "These young men must have known their killer, with them being fit, weighing two hundred or more. The killer would position themselves to make these college kids comfortable before subduing them. As you can see, there is no sign of struggle, which makes me think the duct tape was done after they were unconscious, or subdued, somehow."

"The autopsy shows blunt force on each victim,

some before death, some after," he stated.

"If that's the case, without struggle, these young men may have been sedated, rendering them vulnerable, unable to fend for themselves. Did a toxicity report come back yet?" Agent Barnes asked.

"Yes, the only thing found is high levels of alcohol, some close to alcohol poisoning."

"That's the way the sedative may be introduced into their bodies, followed by blunt force." She paused, picking up the photo, looking closer before taking another one to compare them. "I see a lot of blood. Is there a stab wound or bullet entry?"

"Two gunshots to each victim, piercing the heart and lung, in every victim."

"It speaks volumes of our killer, that they're taking time to mirror each kill then stage them the same way each time. It's impressive, showing how relaxed the killer has become, as if they're untouchable, or one step ahead of everything," Agent Barnes briefly assessed.

"Fourteen steps, if you're counting each victim," Chimentez stated.

"I wouldn't give them that much credit, Lieutenant. All it takes is a closer look, with a fresh set of eyes to see what mistakes they're making, which will place them behind."

"You think this killer is male or female?"

"A murderer comes in all forms, man, woman, child, or grandparents. We just have to have an open mind to see it all, then narrow it down. Now with these young males, a female could easily lure them with visual charm. It will also explain how they're being subdued." The lieutenant, hearing this, is impressed with her assessment of everything. "Now on the other side of things, if it is a male, statistically, most serial killers are male, with three percent being women. The male would be in a trusted position, or close to these victims, looking the part of a student even." She stopped in mid-thought as something entered her mind. "Are these killings the first of their kind in this area or the state?" she asked.

"Right off hand, I don't recall, since my memory isn't what it used to be, especially with all the cases I handle daily."

"Let's check the homicide case log over the last ten years or so to see what stands out. Whatever is in the past could help us out now."

Before he could respond, a trooper yelled out across the floor, "Lt. Chimentez, sir!" He stood looking toward the yelling voice. The trooper was signaling that there was an incoming call, showing urgency in his gesture. "Patch me through to my desk phone," Chimentez said, wondering who was on the other end as he placed the phone on speaker.

"Lt. Chimentez here. Who am I speaking with?" he asked. A recording from multiple TV shows and commercials played. "I don't want to grow up, I want to be a Toys "R" Us kid." They were both thinking this was a prank call. "You want to play rough? Okay. One, two, Freddie's coming for you." Then a more serious electronically distorted voice, came over the phone: "They didn't know how to play fair, ha, ha, ha." Click. The phone hung up, leaving them with this taunting audio.

"The number was scrambled, sir. They mentioned something about Ship U frat house before I patched the call to you," the trooper said.

"Our killer is seeking recognition and exposure, so let's give them what they want," Agent Barnes said.

"Let's head out to the campus and take troopers with us in case this son of a bitch stuck around," Lt. Chimentez said.

"It wouldn't be the first case I worked where the killer always came back to the crime scene to enjoy their handiwork and to watch us to see what we figure out," she said as they headed out, making their way over there.

EIGHTEEN

On the other side of the city, Diane was on the phone talking to junior about what was going with him at school. "I'm proud of you, son. Your father would be, too, especially seeing you've grown as a mirror image of him."

"As you used to say, he's watching over us, so he can see I'm doing right by him." His words made her reflect on those times when he was younger and she felt a need to tell him his father was watching over to comfort him, even herself at times to feel connected to the man she'd love until her last breath. "Mom, you okay?" he asked, seeing she had become silent.

"Yes, I'm okay, baby. I was just thinking about your father as I do throughout each day."

"Everything is going to be all right, Mom. I got everything taken care of, making you and dad proud. I promise you this: my father's dreams and legacy will always be remembered."

"Make sure you keep that in mind when those young girls are throwing themselves at you, trying to distract you from what's important to this family, including school and future business."

"That will never happen, with my focus and drive, backed by the motivation of my father watching over me along the way, keeping me in line," he said.

"Junior, more important, be aware of that crazy son of a bitch out there killing college students. Excuse my language, but you're my baby boy, no matter how old you get. I have every right as a parent to worry about you with all that's going on."

"You don't have to worry about me, Mom. I doubt that I'll be the one slipping out here. Nothing is going to happen to me. I will be safe and aware. Well, Mom, I have to take care of something. I love you, and I'll call later or in the morning."

"I love you, too, Junior. Don't be out late either," she added, worrying herself. Junior was truly focused on one thing, making sure his father's business would expand nationwide and one day globally. Nothing else would hinder his focus or dreams to succeed in doing this. At this point, failure was not an option.

NINTEEN

11:07 AM

Shippensburg University

The lieutenant and Agent Barnes were pulling up to the frat house, noticing the taped-off area. Troopers were already present, securing the area, keeping the reporters back, along with the quidnunc students. "Looks like we have a media frenzy, Lieutenant." Agent Barnes stated as she exited the car and made her way toward the frat house.

"Our killer wants to keep it interesting with the media present," Lt. Chimentez said.

The reporters closed in on them as they approached, throwing questions in the air, wanting to be answered:

"Is this murder a part of the string of college-related murders that've been going on since the summer?"

"Lt. Chimentez, who is your lady friend?"

"Is this the FBI that has been said to come in

helping on this case?"

"Tell us about the phone call?"

All of the questions were ignored up until that last one. No one outside of the troopers should have had knowledge of this call. Maybe the killer himself was the one asking the question. They needed to find out who had asked the question and more important, how they knew about it.

"Who asked about the phone call?" Lt. Chimentez asked, scanning the faces of each reporter.

"I asked, sir," a young red-haired female reporter who looked to be new said as she stepped forward.

He didn't recognize her face from any of the news outlets. Agent Barnes, in profiler mode, scanned the faces of the reporters, the crowd, while listening in to what the reporter had to say.

"What's your name, and who are you with?" Chimentez asked.

"Katie Duncan, I'm with ABC 27 News."

"How did you know about the phone call?"

"It came through to our news station anonymously. When it picked up, we could hear you answering, along with the excerpts and distorted voice. After that call, another call came in making us aware of this crime scene."

"The killer is taunting the investigation," Agent Barnes said, then added, "Let's see what we have inside."

They headed into the frat house as she continued speaking. "We're being taunted by this sick individual, because they're now seeking recognition, exposure for their murderous acts."

"I couldn't agree with you more, Agent Barnes. They want exposure, and we'll give it to them," Lt. Chimentez responded. Then a light bulb moment came as something came to mind. "Agent Barnes, I remember being here over eight years ago. There was a case that took place here. College students later ended up murdered, along with this black guy who was trying to do a good deed that turned deadly."

Agent Barnes was listening to his every word while processing the victim before her, bound to a chair. She took mental notes of everything she saw: victim bound to chair with rope around ankles, a bottle of 190-proof Everclear three quarters empty.

"This seems different, a fraternity hazing gone

bad, or the killer could be deceiving us, wanting to mislead us," Agent Barnes said.

"They could have gotten bored with the way they were killing," he responded.

"No, the scar right there is consistent with the others." She squatted down to get a closer look at the victim. She even started talking to the lifeless victim as if to get a response from him; however, this was all a part of her process. "What happened to you, young man? Give me some clues as to who would do such a thing to you and the others. I can tell you didn't want to be here, with the fight you put up. The ripped shirt tells me this."

"Agent Barnes, I swear if he responds to you, I'm running the hell out of here, if I don't have a heart attack first," Lt. Chimentez said, still focusing on the victim.

She gave a brief smile, knowing her unusual style of processing a scene could shock most people. "You would really leave me by myself, Lieutenant?"

"I would hope and think you would be running too," he said, smiling, then added, "What do you think the motive is?"

He wanted to know how she thought and processed a crime scene. Before she could respond, his cell phone rang.

"Chimentez here, talk to me."

"Sir, this is Trooper West. I have that information you requested."

"Give it to me."

"Sir, in 1985, John Davis Sr. was murdered by frat kids, who later ended up murdered, in the same fashion as the recent serial murders."

"Thank you, Trooper West. It confirms what I was telling Agent Barnes." He ended the call, updating Agent Barnes. "Exactly what I said about being here before; my guy confirmed it. There were four college kids murdered in this same fashion, now this."

"Lieutenant, does this Mr. Davis have any kids or a widow?"

"Yes, they reside in Harrisburg, his widow and son."

"We need to go see them. A scorned mother, fatherless child. That's motive in itself."

"Did you gather enough intel from this victim

and crime scene?"

"I think; it speaks for itself. Now I'm intrigued to see the mother and son. I believe if they have anything to do with this string of murders, it'll come out once confronted with our presence," she said as they started making their way back outside, where the reporters waited with more questions, which they tossed out soon as they saw the two walking through the door.

"Lieutenant! Was this the same as the others?"

"Lieutenant, you never told us who your lady friend is!"

"How can we feel safe with all of these murders taking place?"

They ignored the questions as they parted the small crowd of reporters. Agent Barnes's mind was racing, assessing it all. From the moment she stepped foot inside the barracks, her profiling gift kicked in, wanting to find every detail that would close this case.

TWENTY

L t. Chimentez, along with Agent Barnes, was just pulling up to Diane Davis's residence.

"What are the odds of this mother and son being the serial killers?" Lt. Chimentez asked as they exited the car walking to the door.

"Fifty-fifty until I assess her," she responded, knowing motive is one thing, and proving it by connecting the pieces together was what she went on. They knocked on the door. Diane was already coming toward the door, having heard the car pulling into her driveway.

"What brings you two to my home?" Diane asked after opening the door.

"We would like to ask you a few questions if you don't mind," Lt. Chimentez responded.

"Is my son, okay?" she asked, becoming worried.

"We would hope so. We came simply for a few

questions," he responded.

"What type of questions?" she asked.

"In regard to these homicides that've been going on, concerning some small details, nothing more," Chimentez said.

She searched his eyes and body language, hoping he wasn't trying to open up the pain from the past with her husband's murder. "Come on in. My house is a little out of order since I was in the middle of cleaning," she stated as they entered. The lavish home with attention to detail was also very clean, unlike she stated. It may not have been cleaned to her liking, but it was visibly perfect to the lieutenant and Agent Barnes.

"Your home is very beautiful," Agent Barnes said. "The detail, from what I see, is amazing."

"Thank you. What did you say your name is?"

"Agent Barnes," she said, sitting down on the love seat across from Diane. "I'll get straight to it. Where here about the recent string of murders that mirror your husband's death."

"I did see all of that in the news in between cleaning. As for details, I didn't pay much attention to how they died. Why would someone want to do this?" Diane stated.

"Why? With as many homicides as have occurred, someone is clearly pissed off at the world."

"I hope you're not implying I'm the one pissed off at the world," Diane responded, staring at him intently.

Agent Barnes stayed quiet yet remained observant of Diane's moves and responses.

"I'm not implying anything, but if you know anything about these murders or who could be responsible, it would be nice if you told us now, instead of us having to come back when we find out."

"You're simple, to think I would know who would want to do this. If I didn't know better, I would think you're assuming because my husband was murdered, I would be the prime suspect. I'm not, sorry to disappoint you."

"Okay, what about your son? Where is he at now?"

"My son has nothing to do with this, you son of a bitch, coming into my home with these outrageous questions and accusations. I'll have a lawyer all over you for defamation of character, pain, and anguish! I went through enough when I lost my husband! He was my everything!" Diane snapped.

At the same time, Lt. Chimentez realized he had messed up his approach.

"I would like you two to leave now!" she added, standing up, staring at the lieutenant with fire in her eyes. The burning murderous look that was piercing made them see and feel her anger. Agent Barnes was now standing, along with the lieutenant. She didn't agree with the lieutenant's approach; it was wrong. Now it would set them back, and place Diane on high alert if she or her son was the killer. Diane slammed the front door as they exited, angered by their encounter.

TWENTY-ONE

Once in the car Agent, Barnes expressed her views to Chimentez. "Your approach is a little abrasive and direct," she said, making eye contact with him. "I don't think she should be the one we're focusing our attention on. She felt her pain long ago; besides, those responsible are dead."

"I don't think we should just turn our backs on her because she's attempting to convince us that she's not wishing to avenge her husband's murder," Lt. Chimentez stated.

"The one that has the obvious motive isn't always the one to lock onto. That's how you miss the opportunity to catch the real killer," she said, fastening her seatbelt.

"You're the profiler, so what's your take on the son?"

"We can talk to him before I make any assessment. As for Mrs. Davis, it's not in her. I can tell from how bothered she was by our presence, then when we asked if her son was okay. These things brought a memory of pain back to her about the day she was told her husband was murdered. Besides, she wouldn't have waited eight years to commit murder; that reminds her of her pain," Agent Barnes explained. "That makes me look at her son, then, who lost his father and best friend. He's also college-age now." They continued the discussion of who should be questioned next, at the same time driving toward the downtown Hilton, where Agent Barnes would be staying while assisting to close this case. Once in front of the hotel, the conversation that seemed like a debate came to an end. He would never close this case on his own, she's thought.

"After you sleep on it, Agent Barnes, we'll figure out how to bring this to a close, instead of chasing our own tail, not knowing where to really look."

"We just have to look closer, think smarter than our killer, which will allow us to stay ahead, instead of behind them."

"Call me as soon as you're ready to be picked up. You don't need to catch a cab to the barracks; it's a waste of taxpayers' money," he said with a smile.

"See you then. Drive safe, Lieutenant."

"I always drive safe; fifty-five, stay alive," he responded, making her laugh as she turned and strutted her beauty into the hotel. He was looking on, appreciating working with her. She was also easy on the eyes, he thought before driving off. He made his way home to his split-level house that sat on a well-maintained acre landscape. He stayed up, sipping his black coffee, watching old recordings from 1985 to 1986, even the recent ones connected to this string of murders. Something didn't sit right with him. He came across something that seemed to stand out to him, making him pause the video.

"Timing is everything," he said, looking at the screen before standing up and pacing back and forth. The killer, now knowing who all the investigative players are, now had an advantage. Having this FBI lady come in only added excitement, intriguing this killer even more. It was like a game of cat and mouse, having someone chasing behind them. The adrenaline rush this killer had each time murdering would now be enhanced with the thoughts of being caught or chased by the police and their FBI profiler friend.

TWENTY-TWO

8:00 AM

The next morning, Agent Barnes was asleep in her hotel room, until she was awakened by the ringing of the phone at her bedside on the nightstand. It seemed too close to her ear, jolting her out of a dream. She glanced over at the clock by the phone, seeing the time. Instinctively, she thought it was Lt. Chimentez getting her ready for the day ahead, until she answered the phone. "Agent Barnes here." Nothing, no one spoke, only heavy breathing. "Hello?"

"Hi, I'm Chucky, wanna plaaaay?" a distorted tone came through the phone, making her body tense up, followed by a dose of adrenaline surging through her body, the equivalent of her morning cups of coffee. She wanted to know how this caller got her information, how they knew she was here. Only the bureau and PA troopers knew of this information, unless they were being followed yesterday. "Who the hell is this? How did you know I was here?" she questioned. It was haunting knowing they had her room number.

"I've been watching you work. You're not playing fair," the deep, electronically distorted voice stated.

"If you're watching me, then you know, I'm going to catch you. People like you want the attention. This in itself is going to be your downfall, how your pitiful life comes to an end," Agent Barnes said, wanting to stir this person up, with hopes of gathering Intel on this suspected serial killer.

"Ha, ha, ha, you'll never see it coming!" they responded, taunting her before hanging up.

Suddenly startling her, an abrupt banging came across her room door. "Oh Jesus!" She jumped out of bed, taking hold of her 9 mm Glock, checking the one in the chamber, rushing over to the door, and aiming at it, ready to fire, with her finger inside the trigger guard. Agent Barnes remained silent. As her heart rate was up, she could hear each beat thumping. She looked through the peephole—nothing, no one insight. Then it happened, another banging across the door, making her jump back, ready to send rounds through the door. She squeezed the trigger, standing there intently aiming, still silent.

"Agent Barnes, you ready to go to work in there or what?" Lt. Chimentez asked, standing on the other side of the door.

Hearing his voice brought some calm to her shaken nerves. "I would be okay if you didn't just scare the shit out of me," she responded, opening the door.

"I'm sorry. I can see you're shaken and ready to send a few slugs through the door. I'm glad you recognize my voice."

"It wasn't just you," she said, heading into the bathroom to get a robe, since she was only wearing a T-shirt with panties underneath. Being a guy, he was looking at her fit frame walking away. "Don't go blind, Lieutenant, you can't see anything."

"I didn't see anything, I promise," he responded with a childish grin.

When she came back out of the bathroom, she started explaining the call to him. "Our killer called moments before your knock. That's what had me going. Then your knock set it off."

"They must have been watching us close, even following after we left the frat house," Lt. Chimentez stated, thinking it all through. Then he added, "I can have surveillance on your room around the clock if you like?"

"I have enough protection with this Glock, if anyone tries anything," she responded, then added, "I have to get showered, Lieutenant. I'll be down in a little, if you don't mind waiting?"

"You sure you don't want me to stick around for this part?" he asked jokingly.

"Nice try, Lieutenant, but funny," she said, opening the door. He exited, leaving her to get herself together. She made her way into the shower, leaving the Glock 9 mm on the outside of the shower, close enough to protect herself, especially with this serial murderer taunting her this morning. She didn't have any plans on becoming a victim, when her focus was putting this scum in jail to face multiple life sentences or the death penalty.

TWENTY-THREE

Within the hour, Agent Barnes came out of the hotel over to the car where Lt. Chimentez waited patiently. He was appreciating her professional sexy attire. He even whistled as she approached, which slightly embarrassed her as others started looking. She managed to smile to brush it all off as she got into the car.

"We have a killer to catch, Lieutenant, no time for games," she said, shifting to business mode.

"Serious, sexy, and smart. A real triple threat you are, Agent Barnes."

She couldn't be serious for long. She started laughing at his antics of play, as a coworker. It was a good trait, with him keeping a light atmosphere in this serious profession. "Funny, Lieutenant, but on to more serious things, of how this scum got my info."

"Look over there. You see those media guys taking pictures. They have sources, which explains why they're here snapping pics of us."

"It's what I would do if I was a reporter, knowing

that an outside source came into town and would be put up in a hotel. So, they used their resources to track me, which is how this scum probably found out," she said, angered by the call.

"You want to question those reporters, flip it around on them for once?" he said, wanting to appease his new coworker, so she could close that chapter of curiosity, of who they were and how someone had found her at the hotel.

"No, it's a waste of time. Besides, we need to speak with John Jr."

As they pulled off, he stared the reporter down with dark eyes, even with him continuing snapping pictures. Could one of the reporters be the killer? Strange as it was, Agent Barnes glanced back at them, as if she was thinking these thoughts. Her mind didn't allow things to pass by her easily without a full assessment of possibilities, as she was doing now, profiling them visually and mentally. At the same time, she was locking their faces in, just in case she came across them again.

TWENTY-FOUR

Within twenty minutes, they were at John Jr.'s apartment. Lt. Chimentez knocked a few times, having his own thoughts of this kid. "It would be the story of the century if it's a mother and son serial killing duo."

"Or maybe it's one person that's just as sick and sadistic as two would be to get this job done," she responded.

At the same time, the door opened, with John Jr. standing there looking back at them as if he was listening in. "I've been expecting you two," John Jr. said with a welcoming smile.

"Is that right? Why were you expecting us? You did something wrong, or you need to confess, saving us time and questions?" Lt. Chimentez aggressively asked, trying to get under his skin as he'd done with his mother.

"My mother said you stopped past her place in an unwelcoming fashion. Unlike her, I'm open to your antics and questions. After me, where will you look?"

"You don't have to worry about that, because that calm and cocky demeanor you have is either guilt or stupidity, not realizing how serious this is," Chimentez said, staring him down.

Junior simply smiled, humored by the lieutenant's approach. "Come on in. You're welcome to profile my place, Agent Barnes, while the aggressive lieutenant throws questions my way," he stated, full of confidence that stood out to Agent Barnes.

"Mr. Davis, it's kind of hard for me to distinguish if your confidence is arrogance or simply your innocence prevailing," Agent Barnes stated, eyeing him up and down, awaiting his response.

"Innocence, Agent Barnes. I have nothing to hide. There's absolutely no reason to kill innocent college students. The ones responsible for my father's murder either killed themselves or became victims months later to the same frat house nonsense. The only one still alive is Michael Smith, doing a life sentence."

"They're all dead or in jail. I get that, but don't you want to make everyone at the college pay for their frat house antics?" Lt. Chimentez asked.

"No, it wouldn't make sense to me to put those families through what my mother and I went through when my father was taken away from us."

"I know if it were my father, those sons of bitches would be dead!" Chimentez said, trying to stir up something inside of John Jr., wanting to see if he would react out of emotion.

"I guess we're lucky you didn't lose anyone as I have, Lieutenant," John Jr. responded, giving the lieutenant a look that almost read, "I'm smarter than you. You can't trap me with your loaded questions." The lieutenant's eyebrows rose, as if he could read the expression on junior's face. "Those that have met their demise, it was God's will. They got what was coming to them."

"What exactly does that mean? Did you and your mother handle this? You two took these college kids out?"

"Lieutenant, you watch too many TV shows. This is the real world, with real people losing their lives, yet you're here wasting time."

"I think we're done here, Lieutenant," Agent

Barnes said.

"For now. I have more questions we can come back to later," he responded, staring at Junior. They stood, heading to the door, with Junior following behind them.

"Good luck in closing your case," John Jr. said.

"Luck won't be on your side when we do close this case," Lt. Chimentez said, taunting him with the promise of his return. He shut the door, not wanting to feed into the lieutenant's antics.

Outside of the apartment, Agent Barnes confronted the lieutenant on his approach. "We'll never get anywhere with that approach."

"It's how I work to get answers."

"We have too many victims and families looking for justice. We don't have time for the old-school tough-guy approach. Observe and listen, to see what's taking place in this case. Every serial murder case has all the answers to the questions we need. We have to look closer, not at the obvious," she stated, feeling his approach was hindering forward progress.

"I'll switch my approach up. In the meantime, I'm going to have twenty-four-hour surveillance put on the mother and son, in case they have something going on that we're missing," he said at the same time his cell phone sounded off. He flipped it open and saw that the call was coming from the barracks. "Lt. Chimentez here."

"Sir, Trooper Johnson here. I just received the mail here for our office. I noticed a letter from Michael Smith, up at S.C.I. Huntingdon. That's the kid doing a life bid for the Davis murder."

"I'm minutes out from the barracks. I'll take a look at it when I get there," he said before hanging up the phone. Within minutes he pulled up to the barracks. "I want you to take a look at this letter that came in, Agent Barnes. Maybe this Michael Smith kid has something he wants to share with us," he said as they entered the barracks. The trooper came up and handed him the envelope. He opened it up anxiously to see the contents. As soon as he opened it, newspaper clippings fell out to the floor, clippings from the original murders in 1986. Alongside the envelope was a letter he unfolded that read: "I KNOW, LOOK NO FURTHER." He handed it to Agent Barnes to get her views on it. "What's your take on all of this?"

She stared at the concise note that meant so much, but what? "We should pay Mr. Smith a visit," she said.

"I'll secure this ASAP. In the meantime, we can look over these clippings to see what we come up with." They did just that, feeling they were a step closer to getting resolve, or could this be a distraction set in place by the intricate mind of the killer?

TWENTY-FIVE

12:03 PM

Over at the trooper barracks, Agent Barnes, along with the lieutenant, were preparing to take their lunch break, to fuel for the day ahead, until a call came in, halting everything. Lt. Chimentez hit the intercom on the office phone. "Lt. Chimentez here." Static could be heard crackling through the phone. Chimentez snapped his finger, getting the attention of the other troopers to trace this call.

"I can make you famous. Do you want to be famous, Lt. Chimentez? How about you, Samantha, you want the fame?" the electronic distorted deep voice said.

The lieutenant and Agent Barnes were looking on at one another, wondering what this murderer meant. "What fame? This isn't about fame. People are dying because of your sick actions!" Agent Barnes stated firmly.

"Ha, ha, ha. Now, now, you'll see, just watch."

"You'll see when we catch your ass!" Lt. Chimentez snapped. The call ended, leaving them angered yet feeling steps behind.

Samantha rubbed her hand across her neck, feeling the hairs raise, being taunted by this sadistic serial killer who seemed to be watching their every move. "No time to waste, Lieutenant. We need to catch this scum before they shift gears and start targeting us to offset the investigation of these serial murders."

"Agent Barnes, we'll get to the bottom of this, if it means long nights and multiple cups of coffee." He paused, looking over at the troopers that traced the call. "What you got over there?"

"Ship U, sir, a pay phone on the campus grounds," Trooper Kane responded.

"Lieutenant, it is unlikely that our killer will be there when we arrive," Agent Barnes said.

"We may get lucky if this son of a bitch slipped up," he said, ready to go to the campus.

"If the campus has cameras, it will help show us who placed the call," she stated.

"Good idea. On the way we'll grab some fast food to fill our bellies," he said, leading the way out.

TWENTY-SIX

1:17 PM

They arrived on the campus, immediately noticing troopers securing the pay phone the call was traced to. Agent Barnes and Lt. Chimentez were greeted by a trooper introducing himself. "Ma'am, sir, I'm Trooper Nash, first on the scene. Whoever use the phone dialed and waited for the call to be answered, before playing the recording." Agent Barnes was surprised by the killer's mindset. It was smart, but they left evidence behind, which would assist in tracking them down.

"I would like to see this recording device, Trooper Nash," she said. He took them over to the phone, where the phone still was untouched since they'd been present.

"Just as we found it, sir."

"I don't think we'll find any fingerprints, with the level of time and planning it takes to make these recordings. They wouldn't go through all of this trouble to leave fingerprints behind. We should be looking closer at the faculty, or someone that was kicked out of this school or that was effected by the original case," Agent Barnes said, scanning the area, seeing the students going on with their day, in between looking on at the group of troopers. Lt. Chimentez pushed play on the recorder, and everything was just as the call they'd had.

"I can have that sent to the bureau for a voice forensic analysis," Agent Barnes said.

"Sounds like a good idea to me."

"We can also play it over the news outlets, to see if anyone recognizes the cadence of the voice. The killer wanted this to be found, as if they're mind fucking us or something," she said, looking around briefly as if she felt the killer staring at her. Suddenly shifting their attention, a loud screaming voice boomed through the air.

"Help me! Help me!" the female screamed, standing on the frat house porch. Agent Barnes along with the troopers all took off running toward the screaming voice while removing their sidearms. The young blonde was standing in shock as they raced up the step on to the porch.

"What's wrong?" Chimentez asked.

She pointed inside toward the open door. "Inside, he's inside." One of the troopers stayed with the blonde as the others moved in, guns out in front, leading the way and ready with their fingers inside their trigger guards. The noticeable smell of alcohol permeated through the air. This drew their attention to the amount of beer and liquor bottles around. Trooper Nash entered a room, where he noticed someone bloody and bound. This also explained the blood they had seen on the blonde as they entered.

"Lieutenant, in here, sir," Trooper Nash said. They all closed in on the room and came around to the front of the victim. Agent Barnes and Lt. Chimentez saw it was someone they had recently interviewed: John Davis Jr.

"Check his vitals," Agent Barnes said.

Trooper Nash did just that. "He's alive!" he yelled out, shocked yet relieved.

"Get an ambulance out here now!" Lt. Chimentez ordered. As they hurried to get medical assistance, Agent Barnes processed the scene and victim, for visual evidence.

"Sir, he needs to be untied," she said, looking on at the knots and how the rope was tied.

"Tell the trooper to bring the young blonde in here," Chimentez said. They did as instructed. She came in still seeming to be shaken.

"It's okay now. You don't have to be scared, we're here to protect you," Agent Barnes said in a motherly tone, wanting to bring comfort to her. "What's your name?"

"Liz," she responded.

Lt. Chimentez cut straight to it. "Liz what?"

"Elisabeth Smith, sir."

"How did you get blood on your hand and clothes, Ms. Smith?" he asked. She looked up at his serious face and eyes. His aggression also intimidated her.

"I, I was trying to help John out."

"Did you see who did this to him?"

"No, sir. I didn't see anything. I just found him like this."

"What do you mean you found him like this? You just randomly came over here?"

"No, no."

"Lieutenant, take a breather. She's scared, and your approach isn't helping any," Agent Barnes stated.

Agent Barnes, now playing the calm genuine one, sensed something different in this particular crime scene.

"John and I just met, so he asked me to come over," Liz said.

Agent Barnes profiled Liz and saw her demeanor wasn't truly matching what had taken place. She was hiding something. As these thoughts entered her mind, the sirens of the ambulance could be heard closing in fast. They entered the frat house, securing John Jr., giving him medical attention.

"Liz, we're going to need your information for later questioning when you calm down a little," Lt. Chimentez said as the medics rushed John out of the house. Liz followed after, giving them her info.

"There's no need to waste time questioning them. They staged this whole thing," Agent Barnes said, pointing at the chair he was in, then the bottles in the house, the rope, how it was tied. "They wanted to divert our attention from the real thing, the killer. In doing this, it would be valuable time wasted."

"If the FBI's best profiler says it's a waste of time, then it is," he responded, getting a brief smile from her with his subliminal appreciation of her gift.

"We should really go see Mr. Smith up at the state prison."

"I'm curious to see what he has to say."

"We'll know within the first few minutes if he's wasting our time."

"If he is, I'll make sure he spends a year in the hole, so he'll second-guess doing something stupid like this again," Chimentez stated as they headed back to the barracks, where they mailed the recorder to the FBI for analysis.

TWENTY-SEVEN

11:00 AM

Huntingdon, Pennsylvania

Lt. Chimentez and Agent Barnes arrived at S.C.I. Huntingdon, located in the center of the town, with forty-foot brick walls that confined Pennsylvania's most notorious murderers, masterminds, kingpins, and serial rapists for the last hundred plus years. Built in 1879, the castle-like structure always seemed to be dark and cold to those who found life behind those walls. Michael Smith had been confined here for the last eight years, forced to grow up in this concrete jungle. They sat in the visiting room area waiting on Michael to come out. Each of them seeming anxious, wanting to know what he had to tell them. Due to the high-risk level of this case, Michael was being escorted out with two officers in handcuffs and shackles. Michael, now standing six foot three, was well groomed considering he was locked up with nowhere to go. His beard was trimmed with razor perfection. Lt. Chimentez stood extending his hand to shake.

"Here's a face I'll never forget," Michael said as he shook his hand. "It's been years since we crossed paths. I see you brought this beautiful young lady with you."

"This is FBI specialist Samantha Barnes; she's assisting with the case."

"It's a pleasure to meet you, Agent Barnes. It's not often true beauty is sent behind these walls." His charm made her smile briefly before getting down to business.

"Have a seat, enough of the sweet talking. Tell us why you sent the letter," Chimentez said.

"Is she not giving you the attention you crave for, Lieutenant?" Michael responded, taunting him, sensing a slight level of jealousy. "Let's not get off track about why we're here, gentlemen."

"From the newspapers and news updates, I see that you two have been looking for a serial killer, when you should be looking for serial killers."

"Whoa! Two serial killers? How did you come up with that?" Lt. Chimentez questioned.

"Yes. Let me continue to give you a better view. The person that killed the four fat boys in 1986 may look innocent, one would overlook them, since they never killed again. This original killer inspired the current copycat killer. So, if you find the original killer, they'll indirectly lead you to the copycat killer," Michael stated, having studied criminology in school. He, too, desired to be a profiler or a crime scene investigator. However, the path he had chosen landed him here in prison.

"What do you think you stand to gain in having us come this far?" Chimentez questioned, as if sensing there was more to it.

"Nothing major, outside of a line of communication with my family, since it's been a while since I've seen them. My kid sister, well, she's not so little anymore. Elisabeth is her name. Tell her I love and miss her, and I'm proud of her. Last I heard she was planning on going to Ship U."

Hearing him say her name and the college she attended made Chimentez and Samantha look on at each other, flashing back to the screaming blonde at the frat house. Was this a part of his master scheme?

they were wondering.

"Elisabeth is the girl from yesterday, right?" Agent Barnes questioned to confirm.

"What's going on with my sister?"

"Nothing, she's just fine. She'll get the message," Agent Barnes said, standing up ready to end this encounter. She believed she had what she needed, allowing her to look deeper into this case. "If anything, else comes to mind, Mr. Smith, contact the trooper barracks."

"Can I call just to hear your voice?" he said, making her smile, while the lieutenant's eyebrows raised.

"The persons you're looking for has been around this case since 1985 to 1986. I say this because the details of the case weren't all made public. This person had in-depth knowledge of this case. It could even be someone that works at the courthouse, anyone that had access to the case." Hearing him say this made their antennas go up, fearing that someone on their side of the law was behind this serial massacre of college students.

"Mr. Smith, truthfully, Agent Barnes and I hope

you're wrong, because if it is someone on this side of the law, we're going to make them regret every day of life, including the decision they made to betray the honor of being a representative of the law."

"It's only what I've assessed being stuck in a cell all day watching my thirteen-inch television, the window to my world, my mental escape from prison."

"We'll get back to you, Mr. Smith. If we discover you or your sister have any connection to these recent murders, you'll go straight to death row, even if you weren't physically present," Agent Barnes said, knowing most masterminds conduct massacres without laying a finger on anyone.

"I look forward to seeing you again, beautiful," Michael said, walking away. Lt. Chimentez stared him down, not taking to his cocky demeanor. They exited the prison and headed back to Harrisburg as they went back and forth exchanging their views on the visit with Michael along with whom they should look at that was close to original case.

TWENTY-EIGHT

3:08 PM

Harrisburg Hospital

John Jr. was now checking out of the hospital with Liz by his side. "Do you feel better now, John?" she asked.

"Best that I can be at this point. I have a headache, awaiting the painkillers to kick in," he replied, squinting his eyes from the pain and headache. As soon as they made their way out in front of the hospital, they noticed a state trooper standing outside of his car leaning up against it, looking on at them.

"Excuse me, Mr. Davis. I'm Trooper Johnson. Lt. Chimentez would like to speak with you back at the barracks."

"Does it look like I want to talk right now? I mean take a good look," he responded with sarcasm and anger.

"It's about your attackers, I assume. It's up to you, sir, if you want to come in willingly to talk or if we get a warrant for your arrest, if you hinder our investigation."

"Trooper Johnson, tell the lieutenant I'll be at my apartment or at school. It won't be hard to find me. Liz, let's go," he said, walking away from the trooper.

Liz looked on at the trooper as if she didn't know what to do, being scared. "We shouldn't have to talk to them, Junior," Liz said, wishing she wasn't a part of this. "We don't have to speak with them if we don't want to. Besides, I'm not going to sit in the interrogation room while they play good cop, bad cop, with hopes of getting information out of me I don't have to give them."

"Well don't—just let me handle this, Liz," he said, cutting her off in mid speech, seeing she was crumbling. "If they have any questions, I'll be the one to answer them, okay? For now, there's nothing to say."

TWENTY-NINE

4:02 PM
Trooper Barracks

Chimentez and Samantha were going over the case information, researching every detail, not wanting to miss anything. It didn't take long before they came across the arresting officer of the 1985 case with John Davis Sr. "Look at this here. Trooper Holmes attempted to arrest these kids, and he was shot in the the process, by that same gun that killed John Davis Sr," Lt. Chimentez said, making Agent Barnes's radar go up.

"Is Trooper Holmes still employed with the troopers?"

"No, he left shortly after he was shot. He didn't cope well with being shot; it played on his mind, affecting his ability to uphold the law," he said, flashing back to the first incident of his outburst in the interrogation room. He fell apart after that."

"Where is he now?"

"He lives about fifteen minutes from here."

"Just to cover all ground, you think we should go check on him to see if he has any information or details that we may have missed?" Agent Barnes said, ready to get ahead of this thing.

"You have this look as if you're onto something, Agent Barnes."

"Details, while eliminating all close to the case."

"I'm with you one hundred percent." They got themselves together and headed over to Enola, Pennsylvania, across the I-81 bridge, leading into the small town where Trooper Holmes resided. Trooper Holmes lived in a twenty-five-hundred-square-foot ranch-style home with a two-car garage he used as his workshop. This was also his place of solitude away from the city life and blaring sirens, that constantly reminded him of the life he had lived as a Pennsylvania State Trooper. No one had seen the trooper since he resigned years ago.

THIRTY

Once they pulled up to Trooper Holmes's house, they could see he was inside his garage at the workstation. Hearing the car stop in front of his house made him glance over his shoulder before focusing back on his project. After exiting the car and making their approach, Trooper Holmes started speaking without looking at them.

"So, what brings you two to this side of the river?" he asked in his deep, bass-filled voice.

"We would like to ask you a few questions about the 1985 incident, where you were shot," Samantha said.

"Those young kids, it was sad what happened to them. Now the one that shot me, I forgave him. He later left at his own will, shooting himself."

"What about the four other boys everyone thinks got away with their part, until they were murdered together?" she asked.

"I have no real thought toward it, other than they all got what was coming to them. We can't change anything that comes before us unexpectedly."

Lt. Chimentez chimed in with questions as Agent Barnes scanned the area for clues, along with his body language, when being confronted with questions that made him uneasy.

Agent Barnes noticed a lot of electronics, a recorder similar to the one they retrieved at the campus by the pay phone. "Trooper Holmes, what exactly are you working on right there?" Agent Barnes questioned curiously.

"Oh, oh that, that right there is a standard cassette player. I just fixed it up to play on a timer, to wake someone up. My kids need things like this, to get them out of bed for school." Hearing his description of the device got their attention, knowing it's what the killer was using. "Fixed a few for Jeff Jackson. You know Jeff that works in the Cold Case Storage Department. He came by a few times, in need of his gadgets fixed."

"A few times, huh? So did he specify his need for so many gadgets, as you say, fixed?" Agent Barnes questioned.

"Everyone I worked with knows I have a love

and passion for electronics. It's my hobby."

"We have to leave now," Chimentez said, running back to the car.

"We'll be back to speak with you again, sir," Barnes said, following his lead and rushing to the car.

As soon as they got in, Chimentez mashed the gas, making the tires screech as he flipped the dash light on. At the same time, he called Trooper Johnson, back at the barracks. "Johnson, I need you to tell me if Jeff Jackson in the Cold Case Department showed up?"

"One second, sir, let me check," he responded, tapping the keys on the computer.

"He's here, sir. He clocked in at eight this morning. You want me to give him a message?"

"No, no, I'll speak with him when I get there," he said, abruptly ending the call to tell Agent Barnes what he was thinking. "From what Trooper Holmes told us, along with Jeff being at the barracks during the 1985 case, he fits your profile of this killer. He stands five foot ten, is easily overlooked, being a loner, is very studious looking, and is a perfectionist with the files, stays to himself, need I say more?"

126

"He sounds like our guy. I can't wait to speak with him face-to-face to know more," she stated. It didn't take long before they pulled up to the trooper barracks. They exited the car at the same time Lt. Chimentez's cell phone sounded off. A part of him was so focused on heading into the barracks, he wasn't going to answer it, but he did, placing it on intercom. "Chimentez here, make it fast."

"You're getting closer and closer," the distorted electronic voice stated, taunting him.

"You think this is a fucking game? When you're frying in the electric chair, or upstate being somebody's bitch, you won't think it's a game!"

"Ha, ha, ha, you'll never catch me. I'm smarter than you." The call abruptly ended, angering the lieutenant even more.

"I swear I'll put a bullet in that son of a bitch's head when I catch them."

"You have to stay calm and focus in order to catch this killer. Never let them see you crumble or crack," she stated, not realizing how smart or intricate this killer was. They rushed into the barracks, down the stairs where cold case storage was. Each step they took, their hearts pounded, racing as fast as their minds with so many thoughts entering into them, trying to assess this case. They rushed up to the desk like they were running a marathon. Jeff sat at his desk in this dimly lit basement he called his office. He was listening to his radio on the desk.

Chimentez was still pumped from the phone call and sprint down here. "I need to speak with you now, so off your ass and on your feet!" Lt. Chimentez snapped, staring at Jeff. Jeff stood fixing himself up, wanting to look perfect, as he always did, with his studious school-boy look. He pushed his glasses up on his face, using his index finger, approaching the lieutenant with a half-smile on his face, exposing his protruding front teeth. "How can I help you today, Lieutenant?" Jeff asked in an upbeat mood.

"Did you just call my goddamn phone?"

With no reflex other than a silly-ass smile, Jeff responded, "Now why would I do a thing like that? I don't even have your cell number. I rarely use the phone down here. People know what they what when they come down here. I like my peace and quiet down here."

"Lieutenant, bring it down a notch so we can get to the questions," Agent Barnes said, taking control.

"I think you should listen to the lady, Lieutenant, because you're starting to scare me with this tough-guy image," Jeff said with a smirk on his face.

"Jeff, what is your association with Trooper Holmes?" she questioned, to see if his answer would be different than just radios being fixed.

"As you can see, I'm here all alone, just me and my radio. It's what Trooper Holmes is good at."

"What about the cassette recorders? What do you do with them?"

"I gave those things to the big janitor guy, Jim Davis. You know the one with the big arms?" he responded.

"Lieutenant how long has Jim Davis been working here?" she asked.

"1986," Jeff responded quickly.

"Are you sure about that, Jeff?" the lieutenant asked.

"Yes, I am, January 15th, 1986, to be exact. He was the only one that actually came down here to speak to me other than those grabbing files."

"Jeff is your good buddy Jim here today?" she asked.

"I haven't seen him yet. I'm quite sure he'll make his way down here to see me before the day is over with."

"That's all we have for now. If anything comes up, we'll be back to see you."

"Okay, young lady. I'll be here waiting on you two. Like I said, it gets lonely down here," he responded, full of excitement, which was annoying the lieutenant for some reason. Maybe it was the call with the killer saying they were smarter than him, then looking on at Jeff, who clearly looked intelligent. The lieutenant eyed him down before turning to leave. Jeff sat back down, tuning into his radio, blocking everything else out of his mind, having no worries or interest in their questions or investigation.

THIRTY-ONE

Once they made it back upstairs, Agent Barnes gave her views on Jeff. "He seemed disheveled. Maybe your aggressive approach caused that. I have to say he does fit the profile; however, we don't have anything solid to go on."

"I never had a problem with that guy before today. His demeanor, the look he was giving me, made me want to slap the cuffs on him right then."

"That approach would have gotten us nowhere. So, I thank you for not overreacting."

Suddenly cutting their conversation off, a trooper yelled out, getting the lieutenant's attention. "Lt. Chimentez, sir!" He looked over toward the trooper calling out to him, seeing the gesture of someone on the phone. They hurried over to the phone.

"Who is it?" Chimentez asked.

"They didn't say, sir, only that they wanted to speak with you," the trooper replied.

"I'll handle it from here," the lieutenant said, tapping the intercom so Agent Barnes could listen in to the call.

"Lt. Chimentez here, who's calling?"

Static could be heard crackling before the electronic, distorted voice came over the phone. "I am he. There will be none second to me."

"If you are who you say you are, then why disguise your voice?" the lieutenant questioned. The caller on the other side, ignoring him, fueled his anger even more but managed to keep it in check as Agent Barnes suggested.

Suddenly catching everyone listening off guard, a screaming female's voice boomed through the phone. "Help me! Help me! He's fucking crazy!"

"This bitch and her boyfriend tried to mock my work. This isn't a game or to be copied!" The called ended.

"This son of a bitch is changing his MO, shifting to females," Agent Barnes stated. Her mind was racing, processing what to do next.

"Sir, I traced the call to Ship U," the trooper said.

"I need a team out there now. This must be this sick son of a bitch's feeding ground," Lt. Chimentez said, heading to his desk to look up Jim Davis. He punched his info into the computer, and his face popped up.

Seeing the photo of Jim Davis made the lieutenant smile, as he started seeing the resemblance between him and John Davis Sr., something he had overlooked all these years, never putting the two together. "I can't believe I missed that," he said, pointing at the screen.

"Knowing the case, plus seeing this guy's photo stands out to me immediately. Their last names also got my attention," Agent Barnes stated, looking on at the photo.

"He's John's younger brother."

"It explains his motive, Lieutenant, especially with the convenience of him starting here shortly after his brother's murder."

"He should have already clocked in. Let me jot his address down so we can get a warrant to pay him a visit, just in case he doesn't have plans on showing up, having a feeling we're closing in on him," the lieutenant said, ready to make their first progressive step in closing this case. At the same time, Agent Barnes was having thoughts and feelings that something just wasn't right. However, this Davis brother could point them in the right direction, willingly or indirectly.

THIRTY-TWO

C lose to an hour had passed by before they secured a warrant. Now two units were pulling in front of Jim Davis's home on Maclay Street in the uptown area of the city.

"Listen up, this guy isn't to be taken lightly, especially if he's the killer we're looking for. He won't hesitate to kill," Chimentez said before directing men into position. Then on his count, they breached the front door, guns out, fingers up against the trigger, ready to come face-to-face with who they believed was the serial killer. They cleared the downstairs area before heading upstairs to clear the five-bedroom home. They made their way back down into the living room.

"He must have taken off, sensing the end was near for him," Agent Barnes stated.

"Look around, the living room is a shrine of his big brother."

"Clearly he's still emotionally affected by what took place," Agent Barnes stated, also looking on at the room of photos of him and his brother. "Seeing this displays the magnitude of how dangerous he is, being deeply tormented by his brother's murder. Now to assess his ability to carry out these serial murders alone. I can't see it the way his place isn't organized, with bags of take-out on the coffee table, old beer cans over there. This doesn't spell out meticulous to me, as it was from the 1986 murders and current serial murders," Agent Barnes noticed. Silence fell on the house as they absorbed her words, trying to figure it all out. The silence was brief when the lieutenant's cell phone sounded off.

"Chimentez here; talk to me."

"Trooper Williams here over at Ship U. The female heard in the call is Elisabeth Smith."

"Bring her in for questioning," he said, knowing the stunt she and John Jr. pulled last time needed to be looked into, along with this call.

"That's not going to be possible, sir. She's dead from her throat being slashed."

"Let me know if you come across anything else," he said, ending the call before relaying it to Agent Barnes. "Liz Smith had her throat slashed, killing her. She's the girl screaming over the phone." Lt. Chimentez's phone sounded off again.

"You're quite famous today, Lieutenant," Agent Barnes said as he answered the call, on speakerphone so he didn't have to relay everything.

"Talk to me."

"Sir, the call with the girl was recorded. It's being assessed by the coroner. She's been dead for over four hours now. That's what I have for you. I hope it helps your case, sir."

"It does. We thank you, trooper," he said, hanging up.

"It has to be two different killers. Something in my gut is telling me this. Two separate two-man teams pulling off these murders."

"Jesus Christ, Agent Barnes! This means we have to track four separate people down. Imagine explaining that to the press and the fear it will put in the public, especially if we don't catch them all at the same time."

"It's just my gut feeling, a theory I have unfolding inside my mind."

"You should contain some of those thoughts,

because it got me revved up, thinking we just took ten steps back instead of forward."

"To appease my thoughts, we should look around this house for evidence that may blatantly connect Mr. Jim Davis to the current or previous serial killings," Agent Barnes stated.

"All right, men, everybody take a room, and turn it upside down. Anything that stands out to you, call out to me or Agent Barnes," Chimentez said, heading up the stairs to search, ready to find something while staying alert, being even more ready to come face-to-face with this killer.

THIRTY-THREE

After Chimentez and Agent Barnes left the house, the troopers continued searching the house, flipping everything, the drawers, kitchen cabinets, closets, bathroom, and more. Trooper Mitchell made his way into Jim's bedroom. Everything was tossed around and shuffled around on the dresser. He looked through the papers for clues. Nothing. He opened the large closet, where work uniforms hung, along with regular clothing. Nothing. He turned to head out of the bedroom, when suddenly, Jim Davis slid from behind the hanging clothing in a furtive motion like a trained Navy Seal and lifted Trooper Mitchell's neck up with ease, sliding the razor-sharp knife across his throat, cutting deep into his flesh like a well-done steak. Trooper Mitchell tried to scream, but it was barely a whisper. His body was shaking violently in Jim's grasp, struggling to hold onto the life he knew was slipping away fast. The grunting sound he was making while trying to breathe alerted Trooper Alexander in the other room. He came quick, rushing into the bedroom, only to be greeted with the sight of Trooper Mitchell's body dropping, blood spraying from his throat as life escaped his flesh. He briefly stood in shock, until the giant Jim Davis started charging toward him. Right then, his training and swift reflexes to survive kicked in. He removed his sidearm, flipping the safety off in the same motion before squeezing the trigger, sending slugs crashing into Jim's flesh. Jim, pumped up with anger, rage, and adrenaline, continued forward, charging, disarming the shocked Trooper Alexander, who thought his slugs should have stopped him. In the same motion, he turned the trooper's gun on him, firing an unforgiving slug into his face, jolting his head back. The slug forced its way out of the other side of his skull, spraying on the bed. The other troopers heard the first round of bullets fired and were already closing in, guns at the ready, coming down the hall, seeing the body of Trooper Alexander slumped by the bed.

Suddenly, he popped into the doorway of the bedroom, sending fear through the remaining troopers. "Put the gun down!" the troopers shouted in synch. Seeing he was covered in the trooper's blood, the dark empty look in his eyes spoke volumes as he attempted to take aim, charging toward them. All the troopers unleashed a barrage of bullets until his body dropped, without any movement. Close to two dozen slugs were unleashed in a matter of split seconds. His large frame dropped in a forward charge. They closed in fast, standing over the top of him, securing him and the gun as if he would come alive. That's how much fear Jim Davis instilled in them just now.

"Jesus Christ! I didn't think he was going to stop!" Trooper Hamilton said, moving past him into the bedroom and seeing his fallen brothers. "He got Mitchell and Alexander, that son of a bitch," Trooper Hamilton expressed, becoming emotional. He exited the bedroom and went over to the lifeless body, kicking him and venting his anger and emotion.

"Hamilton, calm down. He's dead already!" Trooper Miles said before calling up the lieutenant. He picked up immediately, thinking his men had found something. "Talk to me."

"Sir, Jim Davis was here. He killed two of our guys before we put him down," Trooper Miles said.

The lieutenant felt bad that he left his men behind, as if his presence would have prevented it. "Pull it together, secure the scene. We'll notify those trooper's families. Comb the house for every detail that can connect him to all the serial murders. Get back to me later with information," he said, ending the call before making Samantha aware of what took place. "Jim Davis was in the house the entire time. He killed two of my guys. This is not good, Agent Barnes."

"Sorry about your men, Lieutenant. Now with him out of the equation, we can focus on connecting him to the other person, the one who fits my profile," Agent Barnes said as they entered the barracks and headed back downstairs to see Mr. Jeff Jackson.

As soon as they got downstairs, they could hear classical music blaring loudly. "Jeff! Jeff! Are you back there?" the lieutenant yelled out as he stood on the other side of the secured cage area where the files were stored. Nothing. No answer. A few minutes passed by before the lieutenant used his key to unlock the cage door. Then he turned the radio down before calling out to Jeff again. "Jeff, I need to speak with you, my friend!" Nothing but silence, with bad vibes that made them remove their sidearms, especially after what just took place with Jim Davis. They didn't want to take any unnecessary risk, knowing they were dealing with an intricate mindset, a potential serial killer.

The silence abruptly ended with the sound of a recorder being played, with the distorted voice. "I figured you would be back. Now you're a step closer to being famous, Lieutenant." After the distorted voice played, a young female voice could be heard taunting them. "You're getting closer, and closer, warmer and warmer." A childish giggle followed, then silence once again. This time their hearts were pounding with each step they took. Even their body temperatures seemed to be rising by the second. They closed in on the hissing sound of the recorder that was wedged in between files. He extended his hand cautiously in case the recorder was somehow booby-trapped. As soon as he took hold of the recorder, the radio in the front of the cage was turned up, blaring as it was when they entered. This gave them a jolt of fear, forcing them to race toward the front of the cage.

"That sneaky son of a bitch!" Agent Barnes stated, running toward the front. As soon as they closed in on the cage entrance, they could see Jeff locking it while looking on at her approaching fast.

"I wish I could stay, beautiful," Jeff said with a sapient smile. "But the good lieutenant seems a bit angered at this time, so maybe later," he said before taking off running.

Chimentez thrust his foot into the cage door a few times before it swung open. He ran as fast as he could up the stairs to the main floor. "Did anyone see that son of a bitch come through here?" Lt. Chimentez shouted out, getting everyone's attention.

"Jeff Jackson, did anyone see him in a hurry to leave?" Everyone shook their heads no. Jeff calmly walked out unnoticed as he'd done for years working here, a real Mr. Nobody. This angered him even more as he rushed toward the front door looking out across the parking lot full of cars. Only one moving car was leaving. Jeff looked toward the lieutenant with a taunting smile as he mashed the gas, making his escape.

At the same time, the lieutenant called it in, to track him and his car. "We were so close, Agent Barnes."

"We'll get him. His level of intelligence will eventually fail him, with his arrogance and taunting."

"We can plaster his face all over the news, state, local, and nationwide. He won't have anywhere to run," the lieutenant stated.

"We have to move fast, before he gets ahead of us and changes his appearance and location. We have to not only think like he does, but also many moves ahead of him."

"I'm shocked I overlooked him all these years."

"The majority of serial killers are trusted people who don't stand out, nor do they seek to be noticed. Some get caught; others take their secrets to the grave."

"He won't be taking any secrets to the grave when we catch him," he responded, heading into the barracks to get a warrant, filing an APB on Jeff Jackson and his black Honda Accord.

THIRTY-FOUR

An hour passed by before the warrant was secured, allowing the lieutenant, Agent Barnes, along with a team of troopers, to close in on Jeff Jackson's midtown home. As soon as they entered his home, they could see the attention to detail, as if his entire house was a showroom for a furniture store. "Be careful, everyone. We can't afford to lose any more officers today," Chimentez said. The furniture, all white, flowed with the white painted walls and curtains. Even the lamps on each side of the couch were white. All of the furniture seemed untouched, as if it was only for show. Even in the kitchen, the sponges were still in plastic, looking new. The Dawn liquid soap also appeared to be new. Nothing was out of place. All items were in the cabinets in alphabetical order, displaying even more obsession for detail. Most people would have a junk drawer in the kitchen, with coupons or receipts. Not Jeff. Anything with numbers or dates, he could retain to memory. He could read an instruction manual once, then recite verbatim every word, even page numbers. This allowed him to alleviate all the books he'd read instead of keeping them around.

"Look in this guy's closet. He has brand new T-shirts by the dozens," one of the troopers said.

"You notice all of the pictures in this house are photos that came with the frames. No personal photos of himself or any family or friends, simply images of what he views as perfection in these people," Agent Barnes stated.

"He probably killed all of his family and friends," Chimentez responded.

"No, he just distances himself from them, or the other way around. This allows him to be disconnected from any real emotions that will hinder him or his movements," Agent Barnes assessed as she was looking around for something that would point them in the right direction to find him or where he would be going next, knowing his face would be plastered across every news station and newspaper.

Suddenly shifting their attention, the cordless phone in the living room sounded off. Agent Barnes already had her hunch on who the caller was. Jeff

Jackson was taunting them, without question. His level of genius allowed him be this confident. "Don't answer. It's him, which means he's close by watching his house, knowing we breached the door," Agent Barnes stated. No one answered the phone, allowing it to ring. Then it stopped. Everyone around looked in silence, not knowing what to do. Chimentez looked at his cell phone on his hip, in case Jeff decided to call it. He didn't, and the house phone sounded off again. "Answer the phone, Lieutenant," she said, now thinking Jeff never called the lieutenant's cell phone, which meant there was a killer out there using the electronic method too. He picked up the phone. Before he could announce himself, he could hear Jeff's sadistic yet tormenting giggle coming through the phone.

"I know you're at my house with the beautiful Samantha Barnes. She's so nice to look at. I know she told you not to answer the phone. It's her way of seeing who's been calling your phone. She's good and will figure it all out," Jeff said, snickering into the phone.

"You're not as smart as you think, Jeff. I will

catch you, you sick son of a bitch!" Chimentez stated.

"Truth be told, Lieutenant, there's a copycat out there. I'm quite sure you two figured this out already. The fake copycat wants to be me. However, they never will be. Maybe you already know who it is, Lieutenant, because I do."

"Listen, jerk off! You're the only one we're focused on. The rest will follow!"

"You speak as if you're in control, Lieutenant. You're not smart enough, so calm down. Now Samantha was so close when you guys came the first time, I could see it in her eyes. It gave me a rush knowing we were so close," he stated, taunting him.

"Your face will be on every news network and newspaper before the day is over with. Now see if you can get away from that."

"Lieutenant, you know if it wasn't for the piece-of-shit copycat wanting to be me, I would still be living a normal life where no one seems to notice me, other than my good friend Jim Davis. I helped him get justice. Everything done with perfection, an art, most would say, that can never be duplicated."

"Your buddy Jim is dead, so that leaves just you to fall for all of this, even the copycat killings until we find that scum," the lieutenant stated.

"That was my only real friend, so I'm going to make you pay for this, Lieutenant. You won't even see it coming. Now put Agent Barnes on the phone," Jeff stated, getting under the lieutenant's skin. Samantha could also see it on his face as he passed her the phone.

"Mr. Jackson, you were in a hurry to leave without having time to talk."

"No need for formalities, Samantha. Jeff will be fine. I'm not in the position to stay in one place too long. As you can see, the lieutenant wants me dead. Now you, you want inside my head, isn't that right?"

"That will come, once we have you in custody, which from the looks of things, should be soon," she stated, making him look around as if they were closing in on him.

"Samantha, if you find the copycat killer, I'll walk right into your office."

"What's the catch?" she asked, knowing there was a twist.

"You have seventy-two hours to do this. I've read your file knowing how good you are, so this should be easy for you, no pressure. If you miss the deadline, I'll kill someone every hour on the hour, making it very creative and different for you. Everyone will be fair game." He hung up, not even giving her a chance to bargain with him. As soon as the call ended, the lieutenant took the phone and redialed.

Someone picked up. "Who is this?" he asked.

"Who is this? You called this number," the female on the other end stated.

"Where are you right now? I mean, where is the phone you're on at?"

"3rd Street, on the corner by the bakery in midtown." He hung up, rushed to the open door, and looked across the street, where Jeff once was on the pay phone, that was being hung up by the female who just answered it.

"Damn! He was right across the street, that sneaky bastard!"

"He's calculated in his every move. Even worse, he said if we don't find the copycat in seventy-two hours, he's going on a spree killing someone every hour on the hour. We can't afford this. We will have to bring in more people, to shut this city down, no movement, instead of having twenty-four bodies a day," Agent Barnes said, feeling the pressure. At the same time her mind was going into overdrive, recalling all the details of the case that would help her close it, to prevent this massacre.

"What if there isn't any copycat, meaning this guy couldn't resist the craving he created for murdering?"

"Two killers or one, we have to look over every detail. We don't need a set of serial killers running wild in this city," she said, fearing failure, knowing how it would all come down on her and all involved.

"We get files and go through them overnight. I'll take some home, and you take some back to your hotel," he said, leaving the other troopers back to continue searching as he and Samantha headed out to secure files, to look closer at what they were missing.

THIRTY-FIVE

S amantha was in her suite on her king-size bed, looking over the files and photos of the victims from the summer, trying to connect the dots and give this copycat killer a face. At the same time, she was trying to figure out what motivated this recreation of gruesome serial murders. She stared at the photos, seeing the details that mimicked the original 1986 murders. However, they were not exactly the same, if one looked closer. The 1986 serial murders done by Jeff Jackson, a perfectionist, were displays, in absolute detail, that came from planning and being extremely clean. The recent murders looked the same, but they were not, if you looked closer at the photos side by side. She was thinking. A part of her thinking was making her add the Davis family back into the equation, especially with Jim Davis partaking in these murders with Jeff.

Jim must have been the muscle, carrying the bodies, after they were sedated and murdered. Jeff couldn't have done this with the four frat boys in 1986 alone. It also gave Jim Davis peace of mind, getting revenge for his brother's demise. She took a break from the photos, standing from the bed, walking over to the large window with a view of the city's skyline, as well as the downtown partygoers. Any of these people passing by could be the killer, she thought. She looked on at couples interacting, kissing, hugging, and laughing. It was something she missed being in a relationship. However, the job consumed her time, causing her to be single. Every time she closed a case, she thought of starting a relationship, yearning for the comfort and touch of a man the way a woman desires. Then she was caught up in another case. Samantha's thoughts were interrupted when her room phone sounded off, getting her attention. At this time of night, the lieutenant would be the only one to call her since he was up going over files too, she thought as she made her way over to answer the phone. "Hello." Nothing. "Hello, is anyone on the other end?"

"You can't sleep, Agent Barnes?" the distorted

electronic voice questioned.

"Jeff, you don't need to disguise your voice. I know it's you. What do you want?" she stated.

"Ha, ha, ha, ha. Jeff isn't as smart as I am. Even if he thinks he is. I can't be stopped. I will be famous."

"Fame will be the last thing you get, if you come close to me, you sick bastard!" she said firmly, jumping onto the bed to retrieve her Glock 9 mm, before running over to the door, making sure it was double locked. It was secured. Now she was rushing over to the window and closing the curtains, before finding herself standing in the middle of the room clenching the gun, her mind racing, trying to figure out who this copycat killer was. Whoever it was seemed to be watching their every move. This had never taken place before on any of her cases, being taunted by the killer. This placed her on edge: she was up against tracking the copycat along with the original killer, on top of being watched and taunted by this copycat killer who was seeking recognition, from what she'd gathered in her profiling this far. Even if she wanted to sleep tonight, it would be little after this taunting call.

THIRTY-SIX

8:02 AM

Agent Barnes was awaking after being up the majority of the night. What she needed was a hot shower with a hot cup of coffee to wake up fully. She allowed the hot water to beat down on her flesh, massaging her, at the same time processing the case, knowing the hours Jeff gave her were ticking. A knock came across the suite door. However, she didn't want to end her shower at this time, so she ignored it, with her eyes closed, visualizing the details of the case. Suddenly shifting her attention to the inside of the room, she heard a thump. Her eyes opened wide, sliding the shower door open, leaving the water still running as she stepped out. In the nude, beads of water raced over her flesh as she reached for the Glock on the sink. Covering up was the least of her worries if a killer was inside of her room, especially after the call last night. She exited with the gun out in front, sweeping toward the door first.

Nothing. She moved through the rest of the suite, mind racing, heartbeat picking up, thinking about the knock across the door. She checked the closet. Nothing. Under the bed. Nothing. "I know I'm not hearing things," she said, walking to the door, opening it, and taking a quick glance both ways. Nothing. No one. She closed the door and made her way back to freshen up for the morning. Within the hour she was heading downstairs with her files, when a call came through on her cell phone. It was probably the lieutenant, since she was behind schedule. "I'm on my way now," she said. That's when she heard snickering coming over the phone, making her aware that it was not the lieutenant.

"Sorry to disappoint you, beautiful. I'm not the angry lieutenant," Jeff stated. "I thought I would come and join you for breakfast. However, you seem to be in a hurry to leave the room." She heard what he said, meaning he was inside the Hilton. "I did get you out of the steaming water, allowing the art of your body of a goddess to be appreciated."

"You're never going to make it out of this hotel!" Agent Barnes stated, rushing toward the elevator and heading to her suite, with hopes of tracking him. "I'm coming for you," she added.

"Don't waste your time, beautiful. I was walking out of the hotel as you were getting into the elevator. I must say, you do have this sexy thing going with your lips when you're upset, but don't allow your anger to be with me."

"I'm not mad at you," she said as the elevator was going up, angered that she didn't look around before getting in the elevator. Maybe she would have spotted him. "When I track you down, we'll have that morning breakfast in an interrogation room, where I'll get inside of your head."

"Jail isn't for people like me. I'm too smart to be rotting in a concrete and steel cell. However, we'll see one another again."

"Why did you come into my room? You didn't risk coming this close and getting caught for nothing. You could have easily murdered me, bringing a halt to the chase," she said.

"There would be no fun or pleasure taken on my behalf in doing that. As for why I came so close, I figured you would need my help, the inside mindset of a serial killer," he responded.

"What do you mean?" she asked, now walking toward her suite with her key card out. She opened the door, removing her sidearm and placing her files down at the front of the suite as she proceeded.

"I am he, and there will be none second to me. Although many will try to duplicate my art of murdering, it can't be done," he stated, stroking his ego. "I do know who you're looking for. However, it would be breaking the rules if I gave you all of the answers to arrest this copycat."

"This isn't a game, Jeff."

"It's been a game, beautiful, the moment some-one decided to mimic my work. I could have killed the copycat myself. I would have if I'd known this is how things were going to turn out," he stated firmly, clearly upset by this copycat. It was like a painter seeing his work forged.

Samantha came over to her bed and saw a note left behind by Jeff. "I have the note," she stated.

"Then let the games begin," he said, hanging the phone up and tossing the burner cell phone into the trash before disappearing.

The note was brief, reading: "If it was a snake, it would have bitten you already!" She closed her eyes, trying to think of what he meant by this, since she believed she had covered every suspect and angle of this case. She was wondering, "Who could be as diabolical as Jeff?" She called the lieutenant, making him aware of her brush with Jeff.

"Chimentez here."

"This is Samantha. Our friend Jeff stopped by in an unconventional way, leaving a note behind," she said, heading back downstairs.

"I'm pulling up out front now. You can tell me all about it," he responded. She did, once in the car, updating him on the encounter.

"I wonder how he got into my room."

"He's a sick son of a bitch, that's how! Who else in their right mind would do something like this?" the lieutenant stated, upset.

"Look at this brief note," she said, handing it to him.

"What the hell does he mean by this? I think he's trying to mind fuck us and the forward progress of this case," Lt. Chimentez stated.

"He said let the games begin, as if it's all entertaining to him. He did seem bothered by there being a copycat."

"We'll look closer at this case. There may be suspects we haven't crossed off or crossed paths with yet," Chimentez said. They drove toward Capitol Heights, where John Jr. lived. They wanted to ask him a few more questions. On the way over to his place, a call came through on the lieutenant's cell phone. "Make it snappy. I'm in the middle of something," the lieutenant said, wanting to focus on closing this case, especially with this deadline Jeff Jackson gave them.

"Two males murdered on I-81, sir. They're from PSU, sir."

"Call the press. We're on our way," he said hanging up. Then he added, speaking aloud, "When it rains, it pours."

THIRTY-SEVEN

It didn't take long before the lieutenant was pulling up on the double homicide crime scene, alongside I-81. As they stepped out of the air-conditioning of the car into the eighty-degree weather, the humid heat only added to their aggravation. They could easily think of better places to be, but right now they had two victims whose families wanted and needed to have justice.

"Agent Barnes, as a profiler, can you tell us why this case hasn't come to a close, placing a face on this pernicious killer?" the reporter yelled out as they walked over by the bodies.

"Agent Barnes, what exactly are you looking for in this killer?" More questions were tossed out, wanting answers to report.

"Agent Barnes, how many more bodies do you have to discover before you and the lieutenant figure this out?"

Samantha didn't like the question. She stared at the male reporter feeling he had something else he really wanted to say, like, "How many more people do I have to kill before you get it right?" She didn't act on her quick assessment. It did make the reporter take a step back as the others continued on with their questions. Samantha wasn't too fond of the reporters thinking less of her professional abilities as a profiler. "Ladies and gentlemen," Agents Barnes said, getting their attention, "we're close to closing this case. At no time since I came on to profile this case have I taken a second to rest. There are some things we cannot divulge because of this ongoing investigation that we're aggressively pursuing. When we're done looking at these victims, I'll say more," she said, walking away from the reporters. Once standing over the two victims, she could see this copycat's attempt to mimic Jeff Jackson's original murders. The copycat rushed these two killings, making it even more obvious, they were no perfectionist as previously stated. She looked on at the bodies while the reporters seemed to have the lieutenant pinned down with questions.

"Lt. Chimentez, are these killings related to the 1986 killings?" the reporter questioned.

"Rumor has it that there are two serial killers, the original and a copycat. Can you confirm or deny this, Lieutenant?" The questions were whizzing past his head like bullets.

"Just a minute, one question at a time. Now I don't know if there is a copycat. We did find out who is responsible for the 1986 murders," he stated, not wanting to add the fear of two killers being out there.

"Who is the person responsible for the 1986 murders?"

"Jeff Jackson, an ex-employee of the Pennsylvania State Troopers."

"Is Jeff responsible for those two victims over there? If not, then are you looking for a copycat?"

"We're not closed to the possibilities of the connection to these victims," he responded, wiggling his way out of the question.

At the same time, Samantha came over, taking over the questioning. "I'll take your questions from here."

"Agent Barnes, who is the monster behind these killings?"

"Agent Barnes, the lieutenant didn't seem sure if

there are two killers or one bringing a murderous wrath on this state." Her head went back and forth looking at the reporters tossing questions out, at the same time profiling them.

"Jeff Jackson is the original killer for the 1986 murders. As for the two victims over there, along with the recent ones, they come from a wanna-be Jeff Jackson, a copycat, that is sloppy with each killing. This person lacks the level of perfection and intelligence Mr. Jackson has. This leads me to believe we're looking for someone who seeks attention. It's what they were deprived of as a child. They may have been a loner in school. Never assertive, always passive, until now. They want to be seen. They want to be remembered, famous even." She paused, looking directly into the cameras. "Whoever you are, we will track you down. We will reward you with a jail cell on death row, where you belong." Her eyes pierced through the cameras, wanting to connect with the killer.

Samantha walked away from the cameras, over to the car, and got inside. The lieutenant took a few more questions before he made his way to the car.

"Agent Barnes, don't you think that saying the copycat is sloppy is a provoking comment that may encourage them to kill more in an attempt to be perfect and not sloppy? It sounds to me like you just stirred the pot even more, so to speak," Chimentez questioned.

"The copycat is sloppy. You didn't notice the difference? Besides, this will get their attention, forcing them to either stop and run or expose themselves, putting their pride in the way," she responded knowing how arrogant most serial killers can be, taking pride in what they believe is their craft.

"I hope you're right about this. We don't need two loose cannons running around out here. One more thing before we head back to the barracks. Let's go see this Davis kid before he disappears on us," the lieutenant stated, mashing the gas and merging with the traffic. He was now focused on seeing John Jr., checking to see if he was their guy, the copycat.

THIRTY-EIGHT

" Oh, it's you two again," Junior said as he opened the door, seeing Chimentez and Agent Barnes. "Come in, take a seat. Can I offer you anything to drink?"

"Bottled water, please," Agent Barnes requested.

"What about you, Lieutenant?" Junior asked.

"A cold beer, but I'm on duty, so I'll have a water too."

He came back out with their water, and both Chimentez and Agent Barnes were taken back by his sudden hospitality, unlike before. "I see each of you checking the bottled water as if I tampered with it. I'm not in the business of killing cops."

"So what killing business are you in?" Lt. Chimentez questioned, looking on at him with a dark stare.

"I'm not in the killing business at all. Nice attempt to twist my words around. Anyway, what brings you two back?"

"Your antics, staging fake crime scenes that led

to your lady friend getting killed."

"It was all her idea. She and I were drinking one night, and I filled her in on the insinuations you guys were making. That's when she came up with an idea to stage a crime scene, to mirror all that we'd seen on TV and in the newspapers about the cases."

"So, who hit you with the bottle?" Chimentez questioned.

"I hit myself. It hurt like a like a muthafucka. I didn't prepare for that shit."

"So, what happened next?" he asked.

"I was dizzy for a few minutes, and then I tied my legs and Liz tied my hands before running out screaming, all dramatic," John said, smiling like it was funny.

"Did I miss the funny part?" Agent Barnes questioned.

"Nothing is funny," he responded.

"She's dead because of that. There's nothing funny about that," Agent Barnes stated. "Now the stage games you and Liz played were also convenient to a call the lieutenant and I responded to from the killer. So did you stage the call too?"

"No, I didn't even know about any phone call."

"So have you met any other students outside of the ones at Ship U?" the lieutenant asked."

"I partied over the summer with students from other colleges."

"Really? You know that's when the first of the serial killings started," Chimentez stated, giving Junior this look as if he was onto him.

"If you two think I'm a suspect, this case will never be closed, chasing behind me. I have no desire to inflict pain or murder anyone. I don't wish any family to go through that pain my mother and I went through when I was a kid."

Agent Barnes sat looking on at Junior, realizing they were wasting time, time that could be applied chasing after the real copycat. "We're done here, Lieutenant. The kid is innocent whether we like it or not. We have a real killer out there terrorizing the people of this city and state," she said, getting up from the chair. "Sorry for the inconvenience, Mr. Davis," she added, exiting.

The lieutenant didn't agree with her decision. He stared Junior down before he closed the door on his face. Once they made it to the car, the lieutenant expressed his thoughts. "If he's innocent, I'm the Virgin Mary," Chimentez stated sarcastically.

"Nice to meet you, Mary," Barnes fired back with a smile, then added, "He may be guilty of many things, but not a serial murdering spree. Now let's focus on tracking this scum down before Jeff turns this city into his playground of murders." Then they headed back to the barracks.

THIRTY-NINE

On the way back to the barracks, Lt. Chimentez's cell phone sounded off, getting his attention. He put it on speaker as he answered it. "Chimentez here."

"Lieutenant, I've been very bad. No one wants to play with me, ha, ha, ha," the distorted voice stated, halting them going to the barracks. He turned around heading toward Diane Davis's home in hopes of catching her in the act of using this electronic voice decoder.

"I'll play with you. As soon as I catch your ass, I'm going to slam you against the goddamn ground with my gun in the back of your head!" the lieutenant snapped.

"You don't have to chase me. I know where to find you," the voice said before hanging up, leaving the lieutenant and Agent Barnes to think about having someone pursuing them while they were trying to close this case.

"As if we weren't already on high alert, now we

have this copycat killer wanting to chase behind us," Agent Barnes stated then added, "This isn't the normal behavior of a serial killer or copycat. Something is off, and we need to find out exactly what it is before it's too late."

They turned into the Davis driveway, tires screeching before coming to an abrupt halt. Inside the house, Diane was eating leftovers from yesterday, until she heard the car in the driveway. She opened the front door and saw the lieutenant and Agent Barnes exiting in a hurry.

"Look at this, she knew we were coming," Chimentez stated, approaching Diane in the doorway.

"I came to the door to see who the hell is pulling into my driveway as if they lost their damn mind! But I see it's your silly ass back with your questions and antics. So, what do you want?"

"Mrs. Davis we would like to ask a few questions, if possible," Agent Barnes said, having a calmer approach.

"You can do it from here," Diane responded, not welcoming them into her home, especially the lieutenant, who seemed to get on her nerves.

"What, you have company, or you're hiding something in there?" Lt. Chimentez questioned while trying to look past Diane.

"There's nothing to see, or to hide. You're just not welcome in my home. If you want to ask questions, ask away from where you stand," she said, being smart and rolling her eyes at the lieutenant.

"Do you have an alibi for the times the murders occurred?"

"Only guilty people need alibis, Lieutenant. They're also the ones with alibis at the ready. But to answer your question, I rarely leave the house. I do fear for my own life since my husband's murder."

"I understand, Mrs. Davis," Samantha said before adding, "We have cleared your son of any association with this case. We're simply trying to do the same here, to cover and close all open doors."

"I know you fear leaving your house. Do you fear those being slaughtered like cattle?" he asked, then added, "Did you at least know your brother-in-law Jim Davis was a part of the 1986 murders of the frat boys you feel got away?"

Her eyes became dark, staring at the lieutenant. "I don't understand how you got this far in your career being so ignorant and blind to the facts that exist," Diane said, angered by his question. "I didn't know about Jim, or anyone else involved. I have no ill will against anyone, even you with your dumb-ass questions, I will no longer answer without a lawyer, because this has become harassment," Diane said, closing the door, leaving them looking dumbfounded.

Agent Barnes was now angered by the lieutenant's approach. "Your approach can be detrimental to solving this case, Lieutenant," she said as they were getting into the car. His eyebrows raised as if confused by her comment. Once in the car, her cell phone started ringing. She answered it on the third ring. "Agent Barnes speaking."

"Hello, beautiful. Have you and the lieutenant made any progress catching the wanna-be me?"

"We're closing in on it, narrowing the suspects down."

"You have to look in all of the right places, beautiful. I'm rooting for you. Don't disappoint me," he said.

He hung the phone up, leaving her to reflect back on the note he left behind. "We need to head to the barracks. There's something there that will stand out, pointing us in the right direction, maybe in the cold case files. He said if it was a snake, it would have bit me," Agent Barnes stated.

"I take it that was Jeff on the phone? He has some balls, like he's on our side."

"He said he hopes we're looking in all the right places," she said.

"The only place we need to look is wherever he's hiding."

"In the meantime, let's focus on tracking this wanna-be, as Jeff called them."

"Is that right? I would like to have him and the wanna-be in the same interrogation room, putting them against each other to see who's the last one standing," he said, smiling at the image of it. She shook her head, wishing he could be more serious and less aggressive, so they could get farther in closing this case.

FOURTY

Within the hour, they were in the cold case storage, in the basement. It felt unsettling knowing this was where the intricate serial killer Jeff once worked, and fled capture. "If that radio blasts out of the blue, I'ma lose it," he said, reflecting back to how Jeff turned it up when they were in search of him. Samantha was looking on at the files, comparing them by memory to the recent files and photos. She also remembered what Michael Smith had said about the original killer knowing the copycat. Then it happened. So many thoughts entering into her mind, placing a face to this copycat killer.

"I think I have what we're looking for," she said, turning to Chimentez as he was viewing old files. "Trooper Holmes is standing out to me. He has motive. Jeff knows him. We need to pay him a visit before he takes off like Jeff did."

"He's an officer that took a bullet in then line of duty. If we arrest him under false pretenses, this case could be taken away from us."

"Trust me on this one, Lieutenant. He had motive to kill the remaining four in 1986, but Jeff beat him to it, leaving him with tormented images of that terrifying near-death night. You said it yourself, his mental state never recovered after that."

"Why did he wait so long to get revenge or act out?" Chimentez asked.

"He was either forming his plan or provoked into this copycat ideal, not to point the finger back to him."

"No time to waste then, Agent Barnes, let's go," he said, leading the way back upstairs, over to a group of troopers standing around. "I need you four to follow Agent Barnes and me out to a potential murder suspect's house." They did just that, following them out, securing cars, bulletproof vests, and weapons. He didn't give them too much detail on who they were going to see, since he was a fellow trooper that took bullets for the badge. He didn't want any of them to have a biased mindset, only to focus on the murder suspect and the level of danger that comes with encountering a murderer.

Within twenty minutes they were arriving at Trooper Holmes's place. The tension was high, having thoughts of confronting a fellow officer who was a potential serial killer. The two squad cars pulled into the driveway. The lieutenant parked on the outside of the driveway along with the other trooper's car. How could this fellow trooper be responsible for the perfidious murders of the frat boys, they were thinking as each step was taken. Trooper Holmes was in his garage like before, working on electronics. He didn't even turn around, hearing the cars pull into his driveway.

"Trooper Holmes, we would like to bother you with a few more questions," Lt. Chimentez said as he approached, walking up the driveway. Trooper Holmes started mumbling something that couldn't be made out with his back turned.

"Sir did you hear the lieutenant?" the young trooper asked.

"I knew you would come back, you son of a bitch!" Trooper Holmes blurted out in a deep, booming voice. At the same time, he moved swiftly, turning around with his nickel-plated .44 Magnum, opening fire and sending slugs into the faces of the first trooper closing in on him. The quick move, backed by the roaring of the .44 Magnum, shook everyone, until the blood spatter sprayed those behind the young trooper, being showered with his brains and warm blood. His lifeless body fell to the ground as the others reacted, taking cover while reaching for their sidearms.

"I was going to let it all pass, until I was provoked into doing this!" Trooper Holmes shouted. Before he could finish speaking, Chimentez fired off two rounds from his 9 mm automatic. The slugs whizzed past Trooper Holmes's head, slamming into the garage wall. "Lieutenant, you son of a bitch! You trying to take me out!?" he said, hearing the other trooper radioing in, "Officer down." Hearing these words made him flash back to when he was shot. Agent Barnes also saw the look on his face, realizing what he'd done was wrong. It was too late to right this wrong.

FOURTY-ONE

He lowered his gun to his side, giving Agent Barnes a chance to talk him all the way down. "No one shoot, stand down!" she commanded. "I think Trooper Holmes has realized this isn't how he wants to be remembered as an officer of the law," she said, looking on at him with a calm expression, not wanting to trigger him to fire on her or anyone else. She wiped her face from the blood spatter that seemed to still be warm. "If you put the gun down, we can end this, sir," she said, taking steps. Twenty feet and closing. Fifteen feet and closing. Her heart was pounding harder with each step, knowing it could be her last. She didn't move fast, trying to avoid any sudden changes in his demeanor. It was already an intense situation, with one officer down and the others clenching their weapons, ready to kill Trooper Holmes.

"Stop right there!" his voice boomed through air, shaking her to the core. Her eyes widened in fear, fear she had to take control of immediately. "Don't come any closer, or I'll blow my fucking brains out!" he shouted, raising the gun to his temple. "I didn't want it to be like this. I thought I had it all under control," he said with a distant dark stare in his eyes, not looking at anything or anyone in particular. He was gone, mentally checked out of his present being.

"Trooper Holmes, you still have it under control. Just lower your gun, so you don't hurt yourself or anyone else." Her voice became a blur to him as he was drifting into a place of darkness, a murderous abyss that had consumed him. Suddenly, his eyes shifted to the fast-approaching police cars, responding to the officer down call.

"It's over!" he shouted, shifting his weapon to take out as many people as he could. He didn't have much chance with all the guns aimed at him. He got off a few shots before he was chopped down from his head to his legs, killing him over and over. They still rushed over to his downed body, guns aimed at him.

"He's definitely done. If he gets up, I'll shoot myself," the officer from Enola stated, looking on at the marred, bullet-riddled face and body of Trooper Holmes. Agent Barnes was also down on the ground, having been hit in the midst of the barrage of bullets. She couldn't believe she had allowed herself to get that close without having her weapon in hand. One slug tore through her shoulder, the other above her right breast. All could have been prevented if she was wearing a vest. She didn't feel it was needed at the time, with all of the officers around her.

Chimentez immediately ran over to her. "Samantha, you, okay?" he asked.

"No, these bullets are burning like hell," she responded.

"We got him."

"So, I guess we found the wanna-be," she stated.

"I hope so. Keep your eyes open," he said, seeing her going in and out, trying absorb the pain, in fear of dying at the same time. The medics came quick, just in time as she lost consciousness. They rushed her off to the hospital. The lieutenant made sure they took her to the Harrisburg Hospital. The remaining troopers secured the area to fend off reporters that came with the rest of the police officers.

"Lt. Chimentez, is Agent Barnes dead?"

"Lieutenant, is the copycat killer dead?"

"Agents Barnes was shot. We do hope she pulls through. As for the copycat killer, we don't know if this former officer of the law was the sole perpetrator. He did fire on the officers here, resulting in his demise." Many more questions came his way before he headed back to the officer's barracks to update Captain Mosley.

FOUTY-TWO

6:01 PM
Harrisburg Hospital

Agent Barnes was slowly coming around as the lieutenant entered her room. Her eyes were opening for the first time since she blacked out earlier today. She started looking confused, not remembering how she got to the hospital. She did remember being shot. That pain she'd never forget.

"Hey, sleepy head, it's good to see you're all right," Chimentez said, coming over to her bedside.

"I don't remember the ride over here. I must have blacked out."

"You did. I guess the pain got the best of you."

"Trooper Holmes got the best of me, shifting his weapon as he did. I need a vacation after this," she said. She wanted to get as far away from this city and case as she could, somewhere warm with a tropical drink, she was thinking. Another trooper entered the room, getting the lieutenant's attention. "Sir, we just received a call about John Davis Jr. being found dead, just as his father, in the same exact location." Hearing the trooper speak sent a wave of fear through Samantha, realizing the copycat was still out there. That meant Trooper Holmes wasn't alone. Who was the copycat? "I need to call the Bureau for additional assistance to close this case," she was thinking, in need of a fresh set of eyes, plus unbiased help. At the same time, she knew Jeff Jackson was still out there.

"Agent Barnes, Jeff Jackson could be screwing with us," Chimentez stated.

"It couldn't be," she thought, knowing the mind-set of Jeff Jackson.

"I'll be back as soon as we secure this crime scene. Now get some rest so you can be back in no time," he said, exiting the room with the other trooper. Once he left, she tuned into the television showing the lieutenant from the interview with reporters after the shootout. What she took notice of was the look in the lieutenant's eyes, his responses. It sent a jolting fear through her, making her heartbeat faster, setting the heart monitor off. The nurses came in checking on her.

"Agent Barnes are you okay?" the nurse asked.

"I think so."

"You've been through a lot with the shootout, taking bullets from the front and back," the nurse stated.

"The threat was in front of me, not behind me," Samantha stated to clarify, not knowing she was shot in the back too.

"The bullet in your back was an inch away from your heart."

Hearing this, Samantha immediately reached out to someone in the FBI, no longer trusting the state troopers or any officer in this city.

"Agent Miles here, how can I help you?"

"Miles, this is Samantha Barnes. I need help fast. I was shot in the back when the only threat was in front of me." When she said that, he instantly assessed that one of the officers shot her, by accident or deliberately. Either way, she needed assistance.

"Where are you and the person you think shot you?"

"I'm at the hospital. They just left to another crime scene."

"Get out of the hospital right now. Go back to your hotel. By the time you get there, there will be agents on their way."

"Thank you so much," she said, hanging up the phone and wiping her tears that slid down her face. Fear like she had never felt in the years she'd been on this job was streaming through her body. "How could I miss this?" she questioned herself. He was strategic with his timing, the recordings, knowing the inside scoop on the progress of the case, knowing how she was thinking at all times. He even knew when to shift her original focus to another suspect or what was evident and should have been obvious. Suddenly shifting her present attention, she heard clapping coming from the other side of the curtain that divided her and the other person in the room. A voice she recognized followed.

"Bravo, you did it. I would have not figured him out with his tough-guy antics."

Her body tensed up as the curtain slid back, exposing the sadistic smirk on Jeff's face. He was dressed as a doctor, wearing the white jacket with fake credentials, even looking the part with his studious glasses. He'd been here since they brought her in, keeping an eye on her.

"I can't stay long, beautiful. I want you to know, you have to bring him down before I turn myself in. A promise is a promise. I always keep mine. Do you, beautiful?" She didn't say a word. She wanted to scream for help, to capture him. However, doing so would jeopardize someone's life. With Jeff being a serial killer, he wouldn't hesitate to do what it took to escape. "It would have been a tragedy if the lieutenant's bullet had killed you. Maybe then I would have stepped in and tormented him, by torturing and killing everyone he loves," he said, not liking the lieutenant one bit. He also had a slight crush on Samantha. Her beauty was captivating, even to a serial killer. "I have to go now, beautiful. Take care," he said, snatching the phone cord out of the wall. She gave him a look as if he was reading her mind. She would have called for officers to shut the hospital down, no one in or out, to catch him. "I wouldn't want you trying to spoil my escape," he said with a devilish smile and crazy eyes as he turned and made his way out of the room. Jeff made it through the halls, until two troopers stopped him.

"Excuse me, Doc, can you direct us to room 825?" they asked, thinking he was a real doctor.

He obliged, simply because it was Samantha's room they were inquiring about. "Yes, no problem. The fourth door down on your left. Take care and have a nice evening, gentlemen," Jeff said before walking away, amused by his level of deception.

The troopers entered the room and saw Samantha pulling the IVs out of her arm. "Ma'am, is everything okay? We're here to make sure you're safe," the trooper said.

"You can't protect me from the monster within this department," she said, leaving the room and heading downstairs, realizing her hotel was down the street. She remembered seeing this hospital on the way into town before she checked in.

"The lieutenant ordered us to keep an eye on you, to make sure you're safe."

"Tell Chimentez he can kiss my ass!" she said, walking to the hotel.

FOURTY-THREE

Diane Davis was at her home; still unaware her son had been murdered in the same fashion as her late husband. She was in the middle of enjoying a glass of red wine when her doorbell rang, followed by knocking. She first thought it was the lieutenant and Agent Barnes back again, until she opened the door and saw two troopers standing before her like when her husband was murdered. This feeling that came over her was instinct, and she turned and placed the glass of wine on the table by the door.

"What's the problem?" she cut straight to it.

"Your son," the trooper said, torn about having to deliver this tormenting news that she'd received once before. "Your son has been murdered, ma'am," he let out, feeling a weight being lifted from him. At the same time, Diane was processing this bad news, and a crushing heaviness slammed down on her, making her knees weak as she dropped to the floor in disbelief. Her heart felt as if it had been ripped from her chest in the most violent, unforgiving manner.

"No! No! This can't be happening to me! Not again! Please tell me this is a mistake! Not my baby! No, not my baby! Why? Why is this happening to me?" she screamed out as everything seemed to get dark, her pain burning like a hot iron pressing against her flesh and heart. Her breathing was heavy and strained, and she was screaming and crying. "I can't live without my baby, no, no, no, not my baby!"

The troopers didn't say a word, knowing she'd been down this road before, having to feel the heartbreak followed by the reality of seeing her loved one dead, to identify the body. No one should have to go through this, let alone twice as she'd done in the exact same fashion. This was more than enough to make her want revenge on whoever had brought harm to her baby boy.

FOURTY-FOUR

O ver at the Hilton, Agent Barnes just finished showering, trying wash the filth of disgust from her flesh. After she did that, she sat preparing to eat the dinner she'd ordered, salmon steak with a lemon squeeze, garlic mashed potatoes, and seasoned asparagus with a toasted butter garlic dinner roll. She opted for a Coke to drink. Before indulging in her dinner, she grabbed the ice bucket and race halfway down the hall to fill it, badly wanting ice in her soda. Once back in the room, she started to savor the full-flavored salmon with sides, until the room phone sounded off, shifting her attention toward the ringing phone. A part of her wanted to finish her food, and the other part, thought it could be someone from the bureau checking on her. This made her answer the phone. "Hello, this is Agent Barnes speaking," she said with a partial mouth full of salmon and garlic toast. Nothing. Only heavy breathing could be heard. Suddenly a distorted voice followed.

"I am the best, the God of this murder shit. I can't be caught. I'm so close to being famous, I can feel it. I'm coming for you next, Agent Barnes," the distorted voice taunted, sending a chill down her spine.

"You don't have to disguise your voice anymore, you piece of shit! I'll be here waiting to put a bullet in your head, Lt. Chimentez!" she said, turning to reach for her gun, only to notice it was not on the bed where she'd left it.

"Are you looking for this?" the distorted voice came from behind her. She froze in fear, facing the devil himself, the murderous Lt. Chimentez. She looked on at him as he lowered the voice distorter from his mouth. His stare was dark, full of sin, the lives he had claimed murdering innocent people, getting a rush out of it. Her eyes were unable to move from him, fearing the unexpected, since he had come here to kill her. She now had to hope she could somehow disarm him and retrieve her gun, to make it out of here alive.

"Why? Why are you doing this? What do you gain killing me or being a copycat?"

"I'm the real deal. I deceived you. So, it makes me a genius, not a wanna-be or sloppy, as you stated the copycat is. I don't need to explain the obvious reasons why we did it. It's done, and we can't bring any of them back. If I could, I would, to kill them all over again," he said, not even phased or showing remorse for the lives he'd taken. He definitely had enjoyed each kill; it gave him a rush.

"You provoked Trooper Holmes. He would have let bygones be bygones," she said. "Then you killed John Jr., for what?"

"He thought I was sloppy, until he was faced with death. Jeff Jackson will never be as good as me. I'm the law. I'm God when it comes to murdering. Who needs perfection?"

"Now you're comparing yourself to him as if this is any better. Murder is murder; it's not a competition. You need real help, more than a jail cell."

"Don't profile me with your bullshit," he snapped in a booming tone that was matched by the sound of a slamming door, which shifted both of their attention. At the same time, like a trained assassin or soldier, the intelligent Jeff Jackson slid from his position behind the lieutenant, taking control of his head with one hand as the other, holding the razor-sharp blade, ran across his throat swiftly, opening up his neck, creating a bloody smile. The lieutenant, now in fear, was shocked that this was happening to him. Jeff came around in front of him as he dropped Samantha's gun and the voice changer to reach for his neck. The fear took over his mind and body as he knew death was closing in on him. He dropped to the floor.

"You're not smart enough to be like me. I'm God to you right now. I own this moment that's bringing your true fears of death and helplessness out. Can you see the darkness of death fast approaching as your power slips away?" Jeff said, taunting him, watching his eyes widen, gasping for air, wanting to live, wanting to kill Jeff for this, wanting revenge, but it was too late. He exhaled his last breath as life escaped his flesh.

FOURTY-FIVE

"Breathe, beautiful, he's dead, no longer a threat to you. I didn't allow this snake to bite you, poisoning you with his venom of death," Jeff said, remaining calm yet in control. Samantha was at a loss of words momentarily, not knowing if she should say thank you or try to reach for her gun to arrest this intricate serial killer. Even more overwhelming to her mental state was, how and when did they get into her room? "You're welcome, whenever you regain your composure and sense to decide to say thank you," Jeff added, being sarcastic.

"I'm going to call this in. You said once I capture the copycat . . . well there he is," she said, pointing to the lieutenant's lifeless body.

"Now, now, beautiful, once I've enjoyed this dinner with you, you can make the call. I believe I have earned this last meal in the free world, don't you?" he asked, looking to see if she would oblige or be against it. She was smart enough not to say no. He would leave, creating a problem she didn't want, especially being injured.

"Just dinner, no tricks up your sleeve," she said, stepping over the lieutenant's body, giving him a few brief kicks to his side, venting from all he had put her through with his deception and taunting. Jeff took the gun on the side of the body, just in case Samantha didn't stick to her words and tried to call for backup too early. She ordered the food, and it came. They sat and ate in silence for some time. She couldn't believe how calm he was, just eating as if murdering gave him an appetite.

"Jeff what is running through your mind, knowing you just killed a man?" Samantha asked.

"He's not a man. He's an animal. He killed recklessly, without meaning. He wanted attention. He ruined my art while blowing my cover," he responded. She couldn't believe he called murdering an art. This only added to his level of malicious thinking.

"I'm going to call for officers to come take you in now."

"You sure you want this magical date to end?" he said, being funny, taking a drink of his Coke.

She got up and walked over to the phone by her bed. She couldn't believe how he was just going to give up like this, allowing himself to be taken in. A part of her professional thinking was knowing serial killers like him, with an intricate mindset, always have a plan A, B, and C. Once she made the call to her FBI contact followed by other local officers, she left the phone open with an officer staying on the line, listening in while backup was in route.

"This salmon is a good choice, beautiful. It has a savory flavor that makes my taste buds smile, but not as much as your beauty I have appreciated sitting across from."

"I'm glad you were able to enjoy your meal."

"You made it special for me, beautiful. Now I must say, since this is our first date, I'm really looking forward to the second date. There's a steak house in New York that has a long waiting list to get in. It's worth the wait, trust me."

"Well, if it takes time, you should start making reservations now, since you'll be in jail for a long while, if not forever," she responded. He gave her a look that didn't match the smile on his face. This alone made her think he had a backup plan. Before he could respond, a powerful knock came across the door, followed by loud voices.

"Agent Barnes! Are you okay? Agent Barnes, open up!" officers and federal agents yelled out, aware she was inside with a serial killer. Jeff stood from the table, sliding her Glock across the table.

"Here you go, beautiful. I guess date night is over with. I do have to use the bathroom, before I go," Jeff said, walking that way.

"Make it quick," she responded, taking hold of her gun before rushing over to the door to open it as Jeff shut the bathroom door. They came in guns out, ready to secure him.

"Where is he?" the agent asked.

"He's in the bathroom. He'll be out. No need for hostility. He's been cooperative," Agent Barnes stated. The agents and officers looked on at the lifeless body of Lt. Chimentez.

"You did this, Agent Barnes?"

"No, Jeff did, saving my life while getting even with this scum. He's the copycat serial killer," she responded.

"Hey, shake it off in there," the agent said, banging on the bathroom door. Their adrenaline was rushing, fully aware this serial killer was smart, with the means of thinking his way out of any situation. Suddenly a loud thump inside the bathroom got their attention, making them want to breach the door. "You all right in there?" No response.

"Kick the door in," Agent Barnes directed, sensing something was wrong. They did just that, only to be greeted with Jeff on the floor, convulsing. "Get a medic here now," she added, seeing him down as the other agents attempted to make him stable. His head was shaking and pounding on the floor. She could see white foam coming from his mouth. He had taken some type of pills to end it all on his own terms, making the great escape. No one had seen this coming. His body came to a rest, no longer convulsing. "So much for a second date," she said, looking on at Jeff lying peacefully. "Check his pulse," she said, not wanting to believe he would do this to himself. Nothing. She couldn't believe he would do this. Then again, he had said jail wasn't for people like him. He could have easily run, never coming to this hotel suite, she was thinking. She didn't realize she was the bait luring Lt. Chimentez right where he wanted to make his grand statement of being the alpha, the best at murdering with perfection and precision. "Well, Agent Barnes, you can take credit for having taken down two serial killers in one night. That will make for great headlines and national news coverage," her fellow agent said, getting a brief smile and head nod as she still looked on at Jeff in disbelief.

FOURTY-SIX

As Jeff's body sat on a table in the morgue, Agent Barnes stood in the Hilton lobby, preparing to meet the press, giving them answers to their questions while making them aware this case was closed. "Tonight, I would like to break the news that not only did we capture the original serial killer from the 1986 murders, but we also captured the copycat, who shockingly to me was Lt. Chimentez. I say was, since he along with Jeff Jackson are both deceased. Jeff killed the lieutenant before taking his own life. I hope this brings calm to the families who fell victim to these two's actions of murder. Now with that being said, I'll take questions."

So many questions came through the air, like arrows being shot from afar.

"How did you feel discovering the one person alongside of you was the killer you were looking for?"

"Agent Barnes, how did they get into your room?"

"Being in the presence of two known serial killers, were you at any time scared for your own life?"

"Agent Barnes, what did you think seeing Jeff kill the lieutenant?" So many questions came her way, and she answered each of them one by one, even giving them details on Jim Davis being connected to Jeff Jackson, then the connection between Trooper Holmes and Lt. Chimentez. In her eyes, each of them got the death sentence they deserved, minus the long judicial process and taxpayers' money it would have taken before they were executed on death row. A few hours after the press conference, over at the Harrisburg morgue, the night shift coroner was coming into the morgue, ready to process the bodies left by the last shift. The fifty-five-year-old ex-army medic, standing five foot ten and weighing an easy 240 pounds, a white male with brown hair, always enjoyed the peace of mind he got working with the dead. Each of their lifeless bodies told a story of how they lived up to their last moments. He saw the lieutenant's body with the slice across his neck. "That's a bad cut there, must have been shaving," he said being funny, humoring himself with a light chuckle. He zipped the bag back up before taking a bite of his roast beef and provolone cheese sandwich, before sitting it on top of the bag, not even bothered that a dead body was inside or that it was not sanitary. He moved to the next bag, seeing Jeff Jackson's body. "Oh, you're the smart one the profiler was talking about, huh? Let's take a look at you, since you weren't smart enough to escape death," he said, unzipping the bag, looking on at his lifeless face. "Yeah, you don't look so smart to me, buddy," he said, turning and grabbing his sandwich before taking another bite and looking back at Jeff. Suddenly, the coroner noticed a sadistic smirk forming on Jeff's face. A part of him was thinking his mind was playing tricks on him or his eyes were failing him. Before he was even able truly process what was taking place or what he was seeing, Jeff slammed a needle into the coroner's chest, injecting him with a lethal toxin.

"So much for outsmarting death, huh, Doc?" Jeff said, stepping out of the bag and stretching before picking the shocked old guy up and placing his body into the bag. He zipped the bag back up before rubbing the back of his head from the convulsions. "That really hurt," he said, but it worked. He deceived everyone watching once more, outsmarting them all, using a cocktail of pills that slowed his heart rate down to no detection of a pulse. The other was to relax him. He took the sandwich and drink and exited, making his way upstairs where he walked past police officers and medical staff as if he didn't even exist. They didn't see him, just as it was before the lieutenant started being a copycat and shedding light on him. Once outside, he took a deep breath and exhaled with a gratifying smirk on his face, knowing he had deceived Agent Barnes and those following this case, outsmarting them with his intricate mindset. And just like that, he was gone.

To order books, please fill out the order form below:
To order films please go to www.good2gofilms.com

Name:_____

Address:_____

City:_____State:_____Zip Code: _____

Phone:_____

Email:_____

Method of Payment: Check   VISA MASTERCARD

Credit Card#:_ _____

Name as it appears on card: _____

Signature: _____

Item Name	Price	Qty	Amount
48 Hours to Die – Silk White	$14.99		
A Hustler's Dream – Ernest Morris	$14.99		
A Hustler's Dream 2 – Ernest Morris	$14.99		
A Thug's Devotion – J. L. Rose and J. M. McMillon	$14.99		
All Eyes on Tommy Gunz – Warren C. Holloway	$14.99		
Black Reign – Ernest Morris	$14.99		
Bloody Mayhem Down South – Trayvon Jackson	$14.99		
Bloody Mayhem Down South 2 – Trayvon Jackson	$14.99		
Business Is Business – Silk White	$14.99		
Business Is Business 2 – Silk White	$14.99		
Business Is Business 3 – Silk White	$14.99		
Cash In Cash Out – Assa Raymond Baker	$14.99		
Cash In Cash Out 2 – Assa Raymond Baker	$14.99		
Childhood Sweethearts – Jacob Spears	$14.99		
Childhood Sweethearts 2 – Jacob Spears	$14.99		
Childhood Sweethearts 3 – Jacob Spears	$14.99		
Childhood Sweethearts 4 – Jacob Spears	$14.99		
Connected To The Plug – Dwan Marquis Williams	$14.99		
Connected To The Plug 2 – Dwan Marquis Williams	$14.99		
Connected To The Plug 3 – Dwan Williams	$14.99		
Cost of Betrayal – Warren C. Holloway	$14.99		
Cost of Betrayal 2 – Warren C. Holloway	$14.99		
Deadly Reunion – Ernest Morris	$14.99		
Dream's Life – Assa Raymond Baker	$14.99		
Finding Her Love – Warren C. Holloway	$14.99		
Flipping Numbers – Ernest Morris	$14.99		
Flipping Numbers 2 – Ernest Morris	$14.99		

Forbidden Pleasure – Ernest Morris	$14.99		
He Loves Me, He Loves You Not – Mychea	$14.99		
He Loves Me, He Loves You Not 2 – Mychea	$14.99		
He Loves Me, He Loves You Not 3 – Mychea	$14.99		
He Loves Me, He Loves You Not 4 – Mychea	$14.99		
He Loves Me, He Loves You Not 5 – Mychea	$14.99		
Killing Signs – Ernest Morris	$14.99		
Killing Signs 2 – Ernest Morris	$14.99		
Kings of the Block – Dwan Willams	$14.99		
Kings of the Block 2 – Dwan Willams	$14.99		
Lord of My Land – Jay Morrison	$14.99		
Lost and Turned Out – Ernest Morris	$14.99		
Love & Dedication – Warren C. Holloway	$14.99		
Love Hates Violence – De'Wayne Maris	$14.99		
Love Hates Violence 2 – De'Wayne Maris	$14.99		
Love Hates Violence 3 – De'Wayne Maris	$14.99		
Love Hates Violence 4 – De'Wayne Maris	$14.99		
Married To Da Streets – Silk White	$14.99		
M.E.R.C. – Make Every Rep Count Health and Fitness	$14.99		
Mercenary In Love – J.L. Rose & J.L. Turner	$14.99		
Money Make Me Cum – Ernest Morris	$14.99		
My Besties – Asia Hill	$14.99		
My Besties 2 – Asia Hill	$14.99		
My Besties 3 – Asia Hill	$14.99		
My Besties 4 – Asia Hill	$14.99		
My Boyfriend's Wife – Mychea	$14.99		
My Boyfriend's Wife 2 – Mychea	$14.99		
My Brothers Envy – J. L. Rose	$14.99		
My Brothers Envy 2 – J. L. Rose	$14.99		
Naughty Housewives – Ernest Morris	$14.99		
Naughty Housewives 2 – Ernest Morris	$14.99		
Naughty Housewives 3 – Ernest Morris	$14.99		
Naughty Housewives 4 – Ernest Morris	$14.99		
Never Be The Same – Silk White	$14.99		
Scarred Faces – Assa Raymond Baker	$14.99		

Scarred Knuckles – Assa Raymond Baker	$14.99		
Secrets in the Dark – Ernest Morris	$14.99		
Secrets in the Dark 2 – Ernest Morris	$14.99		
Shades of Revenge – Assa Raymond Baker	$14.99		
Slumped – Jason Brent	$14.99		
Someone's Gonna Get It – Mychea	$14.99		
Stranded – Silk White	$14.99		
Supreme & Justice – Ernest Morris	$14.99		
Supreme & Justice 2 – Ernest Morris	$14.99		
Supreme & Justice 3 – Ernest Morris	$14.99		
Tears of a Hustler – Silk White	$14.99		
Tears of a Hustler 2 – Silk White	$14.99		
Tears of a Hustler 3 – Silk White	$14.99		
Tears of a Hustler 4 – Silk White	$14.99		
Tears of a Hustler 5 – Silk White	$14.99		
Tears of a Hustler 6 – Silk White	$14.99		
The Betrayal Within – Ernest Morris	$14.99		
The Last Love Letter – Warren C. Holloway	$14.99		
The Last Love Letter 2 – Warren C. Holloway	$14.99		
The Panty Ripper – Reality Way	$14.99		
The Panty Ripper 3 – Reality Way	$14.99		
The Solution – Jay Morrison	$14.99		
The Teflon Queen – Silk White	$14.99		
The Teflon Queen 2 – Silk White	$14.99		
The Teflon Queen 3 – Silk White	$14.99		
The Teflon Queen 4 – Silk White	$14.99		
The Teflon Queen 5 – Silk White	$14.99		
The Teflon Queen 6 – Silk White	$14.99		
The Vacation – Silk White	$14.99		
The Webpage Murder – Ernest Morris	$14.99		
The Webpage Murder 2 – Ernest Morris	$14.99		
Tied To A Boss – J.L. Rose	$14.99		
Tied To A Boss 2 – J.L. Rose	$14.99		
Tied To A Boss 3 – J.L. Rose	$14.99		
Tied To A Boss 4 – J.L. Rose	$14.99		
Tied To A Boss 5 – J.L. Rose	$14.99		

Time Is Money – Silk White	$14.99		
Tomorrow's Not Promised – Robert Torres	$14.99		
Tomorrow's Not Promised 2 – Robert Torres	$14.99		
Two Mask One Heart – Jacob Spears and Trayvon Jackson	$14.99		
Two Mask One Heart 2 – Jacob Spears and Trayvon Jackson	$14.99		
Two Mask One Heart 3 – Jacob Spears and Trayvon Jackson	$14.99		
Unexpected – Warren C. Holloway	$14.99		
When Love Happens – Warren C. Holloway	$14.99		
Wife – Assa Ray Baker & Raneissa Baker	$14.99		
Wife 2 – Assa Ray Baker & Raneissa Baker	$14.99		
Wrong Place Wrong Time – Silk White	$14.99		
Young Goonz – Reality Way	$14.99		
Subtotal:			
Tax:			
Shipping (Free) U.S. Media Mail:			
Total:			

Make Checks Payable to Good2Go Publishing, 7311 W Glass Lane, Laveen, AZ 85339